TEXAS HAVEN

Kathleen Ball

Erotic Romance

Secret Cravings Publishing
www.secretcravingspublishing.com

A Secret Cravings Publishing Book
Erotic Romance

TEXAS HAVEN
Copyright © 2012 Kathleen Ball
Print ISBN: 978-1-61885-344-8

First E-book Publication: July 2012
First Print Publication: October 2012

Cover design by Dawne Dominique
Edited by Becky Hollada
Proofread by Sky Beaumont
All cover art and logo copyright © 2012 by Secret Cravings Publishing

ALL RIGHTS RESERVED: This literary work may not be reproduced or transmitted in any form or by any means, including electronic or photographic reproduction, in whole or in part, without express written permission.

All characters and events in this book are fictitious. Any resemblance to actual persons living or dead is strictly coincidental.

PUBLISHER
Secret Cravings Publishing
www.secretcravingspublishing.com

Dedication

I dedicate Texas Haven to my brothers and sisters- Jim Tighe, Mike Tighe, Maureen Tighe and Tricia Tighe.

I also dedicate this to my Irish author cousin, Molly Garvin Doherty. She has been a great inspiration to me.

A big thank you to Amber Dane, Julianne Grider, Stefan Ellery and Jessica Musso for their great advice and immeasurable friendship.

Thank you to Jean Joachim and her Tuesday Tales Blog Group. It led to my being discovered by Secret Cravings Publishing.

A very special thank you to Rebecca Hollada.

And to my guys Bruce, Steven, and Colt because I love them.

TEXAS HAVEN
Kathleen Ball
Copyright © 2012

Chapter One

Burke Dawson frowned as he spotted a rusted black pickup truck on the side of the road. His favorite Garth Brooks' tune played on the radio. It had been a long day, and he wasn't in the mood to play Good Samaritan. He shook his head, recognizing the truck as the rental, notorious for breaking down, that Old Rowdy in town kept on his lot. He wondered which unlucky out-of-towner had rented it this time. The road to Weltworth wasn't well traveled. Not one car passed him as he drove into town. It was a possibility that the driver had been stranded for a while.

Slowing his truck, he came to a stop behind the rental and got out, pushing his Stetson back. He smiled, puzzled to see small shiny black shoes wagging in the air from inside the hood. The view of shapely calves and dainty ankles looked enticing. Intrigued, he walked to the front and cleared his throat. She turned.

"Need a hand?" he asked, looking into her startled green eyes.

"I didn't hear you drive up. This bucket of bolts broke down, so I thought I'd take a look at the engine."

"How does it look?"

She smiled. "I don't know. I've never looked at one before."

"I could give you a lift," he offered.

Burke helped her down from the truck, smiling at her oil-stained cuffs. She had a black smudge on her cheek that he felt tempted to wipe away.

Quickly righting her skirt, she thanked him with a nod, and moved to the back of the truck, trying to lift her luggage out.

Burke grinned when she quickly drew away from his touch. Obviously, she wasn't interested. He followed her to the back of the truck and intentionally put his hand over her small dainty one. He bit back a laugh as she hastily snatched her hand back. Easily lifting her bag out of the truck, he tossed it in his.

There had been a strange energy between them when he lifted her down from the truck. For a moment, he thought it had been his imagination, but the way she snatched her hand back he was pretty sure she felt it too. Burke couldn't remember feeling quite that way before. Sexual attraction was easy to come by and she was a looker. But somehow, he didn't think it was just attraction.

He quickly inventoried her assets. He had a fondness for long hair and hers looked beautiful. He'd never seen a shade of auburn quite like hers, bright red with golden highlights. It curled wildly, and Burke had the feeling that there would be no taming it. She wasn't very tall; she barely came up to his shoulder. She looked a little on the thin side, but it was hard to tell in the baggy clothes she wore, an ankle length green skirt topped off with an ivory blouse and matching green vest.

Her eyes drew him most. They were so vividly green. She looked wide-eyed and innocent, but Burke knew from prior experience that city girls could be trouble. She wasn't as pretty or as brazen as his ex-wife, but he knew the type.

Standing at the passenger side door of his truck, she looked a bit wary of him. His father had taught him to help a woman into a vehicle, but he wasn't sure that his good manners would be welcome. Heck, she wouldn't be able to get in with that skirt she was wearing. He wondered how she managed to get in the first truck.

There was no help for it. Burke headed her way. Her eyes widened and she stared at him. He half expected her to back away but she held her ground. He looked forward to having her in his arms again.

Stopping short, he remembered that he didn't need or want woman problems. He had just gotten himself on an even keel. He'd get her to town and that would be the end of it.

She still just stared at him. Maybe she hadn't been as affected as he had.

"Are you going to help me up?"

"I was wondering how you got into the other truck."

"That's between me and the man at the rental place."

Burke laughed. "Old Rowdy lifted you up? That man can barely lift his cane."

Biting her lip, she turned red. "I did it myself. I am resourceful."

"What you do lift your skirt up to your waist?"

She gasped then began to laugh. "Well not that high."

Swallowing hard, Burke wondered just how long her legs were. He took another step toward her wanting to find out.

A slight meow came from behind the sagebrush on the side of the road. Burke watched her walk in the direction of the sound and was surprised when she reemerged with a kitten. It looked tiny and its meow sounded slight. Immediately, she snuggled it under her chin, looking as though she relished its softness.

Burke shook his head, watching her cuddling the kitten. He wasn't a big cat fan.

"He must have been in a fight or something." She walked to his side. "Look at his ear. Poor thing, he obviously needs a home."

"I have enough going on at my ranch already. I can't take in every stray."

She nodded, and continued to cuddle the kitten. "Well, we can just drop it off at the humane society."

"There isn't one."

"Really? I can't just leave it here. I'll take it town and find it a home. Are you sure you can't adopt it?"

He knew he was a sucker, but he couldn't say no to those pleading green eyes. "I'll take it." Hell, it was only a kitten. It could live in the barn. He opened the truck door and lifted her and the cat onto the seat. He felt that energy again and it was beginning to make him crazy. He let go of her and rounded the truck, getting in.

"Thank you. I know you won't regret it."

Burke had a feeling that he would, but it made this green-eyed beauty happy.

"If there's a hotel you could recommend, I'd appreciate it."

"There's only one motel, but it's clean and the rates are reasonable. I'll drop you off and call the garage about your truck."

"That's a lot of trouble to go to for a stranger," she commented.

"I'd do it for anyone."

"But you don't even know my name," she protested.

He laughed, glancing at her. Starting his truck, he drove toward town. "I'm Burke Dawson, born and raised in Weltworth, Texas."

She smiled back. "I'm Annie Douglas, from New York City."

"Well, Annie Douglas, it's nice to meet you."

"So, do you go to the 'big F.W.' a lot?" Annie asked.

"The big F.W.? What's that?"

"I thought everyone in Texas knew Fort Worth as the big F.W."

"I have to say that's a new one on me."

Annie pulled out a Texas-English dictionary. "I could have sworn that I had it right," she said, flipping through the pages. "Here it is on page 49, *Fort Worth is known by Texans as the Big F.W.*"

"Where did you get that thing?" Burke lips twitched as he tried to contain his laughter.

"The airport gift shop had them. Why?"

"Did you memorize that book?"

"As much as I could. I wanted to fit in."

"Do yourself a favor and forget everything you learned. We have our sayings, but I think that book is meant in the spirit of a snipe hunt."

"A snipe hunt?"

"Yes, there's no such thing as a snipe, but we like to tell greenhorns to hunt them. It's a little Texas humor. We're a good bunch, so if you don't understand, just ask. We're used to Yankees looking confused."

"I wonder if the word 'Yankee' is in this dictionary?" She looked at him, grinning. "I guess the joke's on me. I wonder how many of those books they sold at the airport." She looked around as they pulled into town. "Is this it? I could have walked here."

"As towns go, this one is small."

"How quaint this town looks," she remarked with pleasure.

"Quaint it is." Burked liked her enthusiasm, but he knew that once she realized that she couldn't get her gourmet coffee in the morning, she'd think otherwise.

"The motel is just ahead. I'll drop you off and swing by Barney's Garage and let them know about the truck," he explained. "I'll have him leave word with Wanda, the owner of the motel, when it's fixed." He gave her sidelong glance. "That same truck has broken down numerous times."

"What do you mean? Who would rent out a truck that keeps breaking down?"

"Old Rowdy at the rental place is a bit eccentric. He claims that it runs fine for him. He blames it all on operator error."

Annie's eyes widened and her jaw dropped open. "Operator error? I don't think so!"

Burke parked the truck in the motel parking lot and laughing, raised his hands. "Hey, don't get mad at me. I didn't rent you that truck."

"Sorry. It's been a really long day." She gave the kitten a quick kiss, got down out of the truck, and thanked Burke as he handed her the luggage. "Be good to Kitty," she added.

"I will. It was nice to meet you, Annie Douglas," Burke said, surprised with himself that he meant it. "Wanda will get you a room. Barney shouldn't be long towing the truck."

* * * *

Flustered, Annie realized that she'd been staring at Burke. He was such a big man, tall in stature with wide shoulders and slim hips. His western-style shirt, stretched tightly across his broad chest, enhanced his masculine appeal. He enthralled her, but at the same time, he scared her. She couldn't allow herself to feel fascinated by any man, not ever.

Annie felt a strange sense of loss as she watched him drive away. She imagined he'd be a good friend to have around; that was something that she sorely lacked—friends. Walking toward the motel office, she wondered about the strange tingling she'd felt when he touched her. Shrugging her shoulders, she became determined to put it out of her mind. Men weren't for her. She might want a husband and a family, but sadly, that would never be. Right now she needed to get a room for the night.

Wanda the motel owner was as nice as Burke described. Before she knew it, Annie was in her room ready for bed, falling asleep the moment her head hit the pillow.

The next morning she decided to walked through town and explore. The main street stood lined with privately owned businesses and Mom and Pop stores. She realized that there wasn't one chain store or restaurant in sight. She would miss her morning Starbucks coffee, but she had a feeling that the novelty of the small town would make up for it. She spotted Hal's Hardware, Penny's General Store, Floyd's Feed and Grain, Julie's Yarn Basket and Wilt's Hat and Spurs. There was even an old-fashioned diner and a church. The town had a feel of history to it and buildings that all looked like they had been there forever, with their original weather-worn wooden fronts. There wasn't one neon sign in sight. The smell of coffee and pancakes lured her to the restaurant.

Soon Annie found herself sipping her third cup of coffee in the homiest diner she had ever seen. The smell of bacon, cinnamon rolls, and coffee comforted her. It reminded her of better times. In fact, she even prolonged her stay. Three cups of coffee was not her norm, but she was reluctant to leave the intimate setting. All morning, families and cowboys came in for breakfast, greeted by the middle-aged owner, Noreen. She seemed a dynamo of a woman, greeting customers, running the front counter and exchanging gossip with all. She was easy to talk to and had ferreted out Annie's reason for being in town in less than ten minutes.

"Howdy, you two old cowpokes," Noreen said saucily to two older men who sat at the counter. She tried to tuck her gray hair into a bun. "Coffee and the usual for you both?" she asked and without waiting for an answer, she poured them both coffee and nodded toward Annie. "Hank and Bo, this is Annie. These two old cowpokes have lived in this town forever." She waited as they all greeted each other. "Annie here is looking over some land her stepbrother just bought. She's from New York City."

"Which land would that be, Miss Annie?" Hank inquired.

"It's on Dawes Road."

Hank and Bo exchanged a strange look. "I didn't know anyone had bought that property, ma'am," Bo drawled.

The look puzzled Annie. "My stepbrother bought it recently."

"Well, Miss Annie, I hope he doesn't plan to be a long-distance landlord. We have enough of those already. What we do need is new blood in this town. Young people like you." Hank took a swig of his coffee.

"To tell you the truth, I have no idea what he plans to do."

"Well, whatever his plans are, it's nice to have someone as pretty as you to enjoy our breakfast with," Hank said, winking at her.

Annie blushed at the compliment. She knew it wasn't true, but it was nice to hear for once. Lord knew that her stepbrother, Sonny, had told her often enough that she was nothing to look at. At twenty-three, she'd only had one boyfriend, actually an ex-fiancé. The breakup had shaken her self-confidence. Two months later, Annie still reeled from the shock, hurt, and humiliation of finding her fiancé and best friend in bed together. It seemed like it only took a matter of hours before their break-up became common knowledge within their group of friends and only minutes after that for Annie to realize that she didn't have any real friends at all. Everyone in their social group seemed to have known, and they had laughed at her naiveté.

The last two months had been the loneliest months of her life. Just functioning became hard. The need to know why persisted foremost in her thoughts. She could not think of any reason why Jeffrey and Lisa tried to ruin her life. Finally, Sonny sent her down to Texas, just to be rid of her.

Annie looked around the diner, feeling her first sense of peace since that awful day. The red-checkered curtains looked faded and the tables and chairs were old, or maybe they called it rustic down here. She wished to be a part of it, a part of this town. She wanted to be friends with these people, who seemed so genuine. It would be nice to belong somewhere.

It surprised Annie to see Burke enter the diner. Her glance gaze flew to his handsome face. His bare head showed his thick curly brown hair, sprinkled with blond highlights, probably from being out in the sun. He looked rugged, not at all like the pale metro-sexual men back home. She smiled as she noticed the twinkle in his blue eyes, a twinkle that seemed to be exclusively for her.

"Well, just the little lady I was looking for." Burke sat down beside her.

Annie grew a bit nervous. "You were looking for me?" she asked, a little puzzled as to why. in disbelief.

Burke grinned. "I gave Old Rowdy the riot act for renting you that truck," he explained. "There's a more reliable one sitting outside your motel room. This one shouldn't give you any trouble."

"Thank you. How's Kitty?"

"Fine."

She wished she had more to say. Her mind was blank and she felt like a ninny just staring at him.

"Well, howdy, Burke!" Noreen greeted, automatically pouring him a cup of coffee. "How's the wife hunt going?" She turned to Annie with mischievous eyes. "This hunk is advertising for a wife." She laughed. "Just look at him. He's got to be the most handsome man in the whole dang county!"

Annie looked in astonishment from Noreen's animated expressions to Burke's reddened face. She wondered what was wrong with Burke. Why advertise for a wife? He seemed likable enough, even helpful.

"I don't have time for a courtship," he bit off defensively. "I labor 24/7 working my ranch."

Annie took his explanation with a grain of salt. She knew that men hid their evil qualities until they were ready to show their true colors. Her instincts told her that Burke was a decent person, but she couldn't trust her instincts anymore, especially where men were concerned.

"Annie, are you married?" Noreen asked with humor in her eyes. She obviously loved teasing Burke.

Annie squirmed in her seat. This turn in conversation was definitely uncomfortable. "I need to get going." She got up to leave, turning to Burke and thanking him again for all his help with the rental truck. With a smile and a wave, she quickly left the diner before Noreen could continue with her matchmaking.

* * * *

Annie clutched the steering wheel of the truck with both hands. The dirt road that led up to her stepbrother's property was beyond bumpy. Her teeth clattered in her head as she drove on, hoping for an end to the torture. Nevertheless, the scenery looked beautiful; she could understand why people loved Texas. The sun seemed brighter, the sky bluer and the grass certainly appeared greener. Maybe she was just being fanciful, but she was really starting to love Texas.

She stopped the truck before an old run-down farmhouse. It looked as though it'd been standing empty for a hundred years. The paint was peeling and the front steps were in disrepair. It had a certain charm though. The long wraparound porch was something from her dreams and the rose bushes in front, though untended, bloomed in bold radiant colors of red and yellow.

Hopping out of the truck, Annie made her way to the house. She had a key, but since the front door barely hung on its hinges, it didn't look like she would need it. Carefully, she climbed the front stairs, smiling to herself as they creaked, and cautiously pushed the front door open. It wasn't a big house by any means. The front room boasted a big stone fireplace, marred hardwood floors, and old broken furniture. Its quaintness captivated her.

Annie walked into the only other room on the first floor and found, to her delight, an authentic farmhouse kitchen. A big antique stove dominated the room and she wondered in what era it belonged. The wooden counters looked well-used, with numerous scratches etched in them, and the sink was huge. People were paying big bucks to obtain this look in their own homes, and here was the real thing.

She'd been so lost in thought that she imagined she heard cattle outside. Laughing at herself, Annie went to the window and to her surprise, there really were cattle out there.

She walked out the back kitchen door and stared. Beyond the barn, she saw a fenced-in sea of cattle. It surprised her that she hadn't heard their lulling while driving to the cottage, but it was a spectacular sight! After all, Annie wasn't used to animals of any type. Her mother never allowed her to have a pet. She considered all animals dirty.

As if in a trance, Annie felt them beckoning her to come closer. She practically ran in delight, through the tall Texas grass, to the fence and climbed up on the first rung, wanting a closer look.

She looked off into the distance when she heard the pounding of hooves. A real-life cowboy, riding her way, mesmerized her. As the rider got closer, Annie recognized him as the handsome Burke Dawson. Her stomach tied in knots as she watched him ride closer.

He looked pure cowboy, as though he'd been born to the saddle, from his Stetson to his worn black boots to his brown leather chaps. Annie realized that she was practically drooling and mentally reprimanded herself. She knew about men and didn't want any part of them, but she couldn't stop staring at this particular cowboy. She smiled like a fool when he stopped in front of her, but she couldn't seem to help herself.

Burke rode to her. "What are you doing on my land? Are you lost, or did your truck break down again? Let me guess. You don't know what a GPS is and you can't read a map." He stared down at her from atop of his horse. Biting off the rest of what he was about to say, he swung down from his saddle. "What's wrong?"

"I...I'm sorry." She jumped off the fence and took a step back. She had learned the hard way just how dangerous an angry man could be. Annie wanted nothing more than to get away from him, but she found herself unable. Burke vaulted the fence and came toward her.

"I don't understand. I thought this was the land my stepbrother just bought. My mistake."

Annie turned and walked quickly away, never wanting to see Burke again. She felt humiliated and deep down, even scared. She just wanted to get as far away from that house and that man as she could.

* * * *

Burke wasn't used to such temperamental females. Hell, he wasn't used to females at all. He didn't consider his ex-wife a true example of a woman. She was more of a hellcat that deserved drowning at birth.

"Annie, wait!" When he saw her stop half way to the house and turn, he hurried after her. It amused him that she wouldn't meet his gaze. "There's been some kind of misunderstanding here, darlin'," he drawled, in a honeyed voice full of his Texas twang.

Annie's eyes quickly looked up to his.

Burke took a step closer as he realized that his Southern charm worked. "Now little darlin', there must be some reason why you're on my land. I know in some circles they'd call it trespassing but since we're acquaintances, we'll just forget about that. I realize that we have a certain chemistry."

Annie's face turned red. "Let me tell you something. I'm not a lonely woman chasing after you. Of all the conceited gall!" Annie's green eyes flashed, staring him down. "I was under the impression that my stepbrother bought this land. I have the deed." She fumbled around in her purse, trying to find it. Finally, she pulled it out and thrust it into his hands.

Burke briefly looked over the deed. Unfortunately, what she said was true. Part of his divorce settlement stipulated that his ex-wife received one-half of the land that his family had owned for generations. He hadn't known that she had actually gone and sold it, and he felt gut- kicked. His chest tightened and he found it hard to breathe. Walking to the stairs leading to the kitchen, he sat down.

Slowly, she sat beside him and gently laid a comforting hand on his arm. "Is something wrong? This all seems to be a shock to you."

They sat there for what seemed an eternity before Burke finally looked at her, shaking his head in disbelief. He'd been working so backbreaking hard this past year, trying to keep his ranch going, and now this. He put his hand over Annie's and found a serene comfort in having her small hand in his.

He looked at her worried eyes and winced. It wasn't her fault, and he felt guilty for raising his voice to her earlier. It was obvious from her reaction at the time that sometime in her past she had suffered at the hands of a man. He sighed heavily, remembering her bright smile when he first rode up. He felt like a heel for ruining her day. "I'm the one who's sorry, darlin'. I had no right to come at you like that. I honestly had no idea that she sold my land."

"Who?"

Burke quickly shook his head. "I don't want to go into all that now," he said with a halfhearted smile. Despite what he had said to her earlier, she was so compassionate and kind to him now. He wanted to make it up to her. "Have dinner with me tonight," he blurted out suddenly.

He felt her gaze on him, taking his measure. "I'd be happy to have dinner with you," she answered softly.

Burke grinned. "Come on over to my place tonight and I'll rustle up some steaks, okay?"

Annie smiled. "Sure, that will be fine."

"Seven o'clock okay for you?" he asked.

"I'll see you then," she replied.

He watched her walk away admiring her backside as her hips swayed back and forth. She looked good in jeans. Too bad she wasn't his type. Her good looks, shapely body, and the fact that she wasn't a country girl ruled her out.

He had a few replies to his ad for a wife. Nothing looked too promising, but one of them would have to do. His time for love was over. He had his chance, and it turned out to be a false chance that he paid dearly for.

Chapter Two

Annie felt like a nervous wreck by the time she drove up to Burke's ranch. At one point, she reached for the phone wanting to cancel their dinner, but she didn't have his number. Calling the hotel owner, Wanda, or Noreen was out of the question. She didn't want everyone to know that she was having dinner with him. In the end, she decided to live a little. Although he intimidated her, Annie felt drawn to that big man. She knew that he could be kind and she sensed a certain honesty in him. That was the most important thing. But she wasn't sure if she could trust her senses, not after the disaster in New York. Jeffrey and Lisa's betrayal had shattered her. In the end, she gave him the benefit of the doubt and hopped into her rental, heading for his house.

Burke's house was certainly big and Annie found it charming. It looked similar to the smaller farmhouse she had seen earlier but on a much grander scale. She smiled in delight as she studied it. It needed a coat of paint, but otherwise it seemed well-maintained, well-loved. This house also had a wraparound porch lined in front with roses, well-tended roses. She walked to the front door with butterflies in her stomach, but she also felt a lightness of spirit. She had a good feeling about the evening.

Burke opened the door, smiling at her. "Welcome, I'm glad you're here," he said softly and ushered her inside.

The kitten from before rushed to her, and she picked it up, rubbing her cheek against its soft fur.

He led her into the kitchen, but not before Annie saw the massive fireplace in the family room.

How beautiful. She could almost picture herself curled up on the leather couch in front of a roaring fire on a winter's day. The wood floors and exposed beams added more rustic charm. From what she could see, it looked very masculine, not a curtain or knickknack in sight. It surprised her considering he was married until recently.

If the family room made her want to curl up and be comfortable, then the kitchen made her want to twirl around in a circle. It looked enthralling with huge windows and it had to be the biggest kitchen she'd ever seen! The wooden cabinets, counters, and floors showed signs of great wear that Annie knew showed the love of the generations of Dawsons. The warmth of family in this room made her wistful for things she never had. Things she probably would never have.

"I know it's not much," he started. "I guess I haven't replaced anything since my father died."

"Oh!" exclaimed Annie. "This is wonderful! I mean I just love this house. The kitchen is magnificent!"

The cat began to struggle in her arms. "What did you name him?" Annie put the kitten down.

"The cat? It's a she and her name is Cat."

"Why Cat? How about Betsy or Polly?"

Burke looked at her in horror. "A man does not name his cat Betsy and definitely not Polly. Cat is as good as it gets."

Annie held back a laugh. *It must be a Texas thing*, she thought.

He opened the fridge grabbed two beers and offered her one. Annie noted how he intensely observed her.

Accepting the beer, she noticed that he didn't offer her a glass. It was obvious by his hooded gaze that he did it on purpose. Did he expect her to be too prissy to drink beer straight out of the bottle? Well, she would show him. Pointedly looking at him, she took a nice long swig of beer. By the surprised look on his face, she surmised that she had just passed his unspoken challenge.

Burke looked a bit flustered by her perusal of him. Scowling he led her and Cat to the back yard where he had dinner all ready to go.

Burke set delicious looking steaks on the table. Annie shrieked as Cat suddenly took one of the big steaks in its tiny mouth and took off, leading her on a merry chase.

"Don't just stand there! Help me."

"Here, kitty," Burke called.

Annie laughed. "Like that's going to work."

Burke squatted down and called for the kitten once again and to Annie's amazement Cat went right to him, steak and all. "That was almost as much fun as watching a greenhorn trying to lasso a calf. Guess we'll just have to share the other steak." Burke petted Cat. He cut her a small piece and threw the rest out.

Annie felt enchanted. For all the show of not liking cats, Burke seemed attached to this one. If only he had given her a better name.

After a delicious dinner of steak, potatoes, and homemade biscuits, they sat on the porch swing in the front of the house. The night had cooled pleasantly with a refreshing breeze blowing the prairie grass back and forth. Long-stalked sunflowers bent and danced to some unknown ballet. Annie closed her eyes and took it all in. She wanted to make a memory of this place, of this moment for when she was back in New York. It was going to be harder to go back to her stark existence after this perfect night. She looked at Burke's profile hoping to memorize it too. There was such strength in his features from his square jaw line to his crooked nose. She wondered if he had broken it in a fight. His eyes were so blue that she had gotten lost in them many times throughout the evening. All of Annie's nerves tingled as her arm brushed against his. There was no doubt about the attraction they had for each other.

"Have you always lived on this ranch?"

Burke grinned. "All my life."

"It must have been nice growing up here with your family."

"Well, my mother was a saint of course and my father… let's see, how can I describe him without chasing you away? He was a strict old son of a gun who was about as mule-headed as a man could be. It was his way or you suffered the consequences. I guess you could say that I was a slow learner."

Annie put her hand on his arm. "I grew up basically the same way. I know all about consequences."

* * * *

They sat on the swing in complete silence. The sky was beginning to darken. Burke put his arm around her, pulling her close. He could feel her tremble at his touch and it humbled him. He couldn't remember a time when a woman had such a reaction to him. The urge to pick her up in his arms and carry her to his bed was strong but he didn't dare. He didn't think she was the type for a one-night stand and that was all he was willing to offer.

Although he found her damn attractive, she was off limits. All he needed equated to an unpaid housekeeper not a woman that probably had no practical skills, even so, she was very tempting. There seemed something so vulnerable about her that it made him long to protect her.

He made the mistake of looking down at her upturned face. Her luminous green eyes trapped him. Unable to resist the pull of her he carefully leaned down and brushed his lips against hers. He only intended for the kiss to be brief, but she tasted like honey and he had to have more.

Annie moaned as Burke kissed her again. He swiped his tongue along the seam of her lips, coaxing her mouth open and deepening the kiss. His arms tightened around her, pulling her close to him. She smelled of sunshine, sweet and warm. Reluctantly he let her go. Annie smiled back at him anyway, and it pleased him. She looked lovely in her yellow sundress with her curly auburn hair falling down her back, and he couldn't help but admire her cute figure.

Gently, he removed her arms from around his neck and looked down at her with hooded eyes. Highly aroused by her, it was by sheer willpower that he stopped his advances. Her bruised lips looked inviting to him and her eyes shone with pleasure. God he wanted her. Burke smiled at her enthusiasm. The last woman in his house had overtly insulted every inch of it. He could hardly believe her reaction. She seemed genuine in her pleasure over everything. But, he reminded himself that it didn't really matter. Burke grinned as he watched her scoop up the cat and whisper in its ear, her happiness so apparent. For a second he was glad that he adopted that ornery cat.

Regretfully, he stood up and moved away from her. "It's been fun."

"Yes it has," Annie stood. She wobbled a bit and made her way to the porch stairs. She looked at Burke with her heart shining in her eyes. "Maybe you could consider me as a candidate for a wife?" she asked quietly.

He hesitated, not knowing what to say.

"Never mind." She hurriedly rushed down the stairs to her car.

Maybe in another life, it would have worked, but he knew what the ending to their story would be.

* * * *

Three weeks later, Annie felt at her wits end, looking around her office she sighed in exhaustion. Every time she closed her eyes, she saw Burke with his regretful eyes, telling her that she wasn't good enough to be his wife. Well, to be honest, he never really said she wasn't good enough, but that was how she felt nonetheless. Dozens of times in the last few weeks she relived their kiss. He had made her feel things she'd never imagined feeling with any man. The knowledge that she wouldn't see him again brought a constant sadness to her eyes. She'd made a fool of herself once again.

Desperately searching for a new path in her life, she decided that she wouldn't feel sorry for herself any longer. Annie rubbed her tired eyes and tried to think of her next move.

She was so sick of committees and fundraisers. Even volunteering at the animal shelter hadn't given her the boost it usually did. She had thought about moving but rejected that idea. The only place she'd want to move to would be Weltworth, but she knew that was impossible. Seeing Burke and his new wife would be torture. No, a new job was the answer and a cat, definitely a cat with a girly name.

Feeling better for having made a decision, Annie packed up her things and went home. No sooner did she have her shoes off then the doorbell rang. A delivery of flowers surprised her.

The man holding the tell-tale box looked down at his clipboard. "Ms. Douglas?"

"That's me."

Without another word, the man handed over the flowers. After tipping the driver, she closed the door and walked over to her coffee table, setting the box down and carefully opening it. Her heart began to beat out of her chest. She hoped that they were from Burke. To her delight, the dozen, long stemmed, red roses were indeed from Burke. Included was a note, "Will you marry me?"

She cried out in shock and delight. This couldn't be happening. Fairytales didn't happen to the ugly stepsister, only to Cinderella, and Cinderella she wasn't. Annie sank quickly into her favorite chair, reeling, not knowing what to think. She was afraid to believe that it was real. The pain of finding her ex-fiancé Jeffery in bed with her best friend Lisa continued to devastate her to this day. The awful things he'd said to her still made her want to curl up and die. He had called her a cold frigid bitch, because she insisted on saving herself for her wedding night. He laughed at her and taunted her with the fact that he and Lisa had been lovers all along. He said he never really planned to marry her. It was all a cruel joke. Could this be another joke?

What little self-esteem she possessed had taken a beating that day. She stroked the soft petals of the red roses wanting to believe in this proposal. She wanted to believe in Burke, but her past held her back. She should have been jumping for joy. Instead, doubts tore her apart. It wasn't fair. Annie nearly jumped out of her skin when her phone rang. Numbly, she looked at it, not wanting to answer. She was half-afraid that someone at the other end would be laughing at her, but she told herself to buck up as she reached for the phone. It shrilled one last time, then it went silent, and the caller didn't leave a message.

Annie slumped in her chair, berating herself for being such a coward. Why hadn't she picked it up? Stoking the soft, red petal of one of the roses, she wished that she wasn't such a coward. She wanted to talk to Burke; she missed him so much.

Annie got up and walked to the windows in her stark apartment. Leaning her head against the glass pane, she felt a knot growing in her stomach. He didn't love her, but she couldn't miss this chance at happiness. Her feelings for him were so confusing, she barely knew him, but she felt such a connection to him, such a longing for him. She would have liked to say she loved him, but she wasn't sure what love was. Living her life under her mother's thumb, then her stepfather's and now her stepbrother's hadn't given her any inkling about love. A life of her own was what she needed. Sonny wasn't going to be pleased with her leaving, but she needed to spread her wings.

Annie jumped when the phone rang again. She ran to it picked it up on the second ring, desperate to talk to Burke.

"Burke?"

"Did you get my flowers?"

"Yes, they are beautiful. Thank you," she replied nervously.

"Oh hell, Annie will you marry me?" Burke blurted out.

Annie knew that it was a total leap of faith, but she grabbed it. She wanted the brass ring for once. "I can't believe you're asking me. The answer is yes."

"Oh good. When can you get here?"

Annie laughed. His impatience thrilled her. "In a month I suppose," she started.

"No!" he shouted. "How about a week, week and a half at most? In fact, the sooner the better. I want you here with me."

Annie hesitated; he wanted her, but would that be enough? She closed her eyes and took a deep breath "Okay. I have a lot of things to take care of. I have to pack and close up my apartment, give notice at my job, and who knows what else." Her mind reeled with the amount of planning and work involved. "I want to be there too. I'll do my best to wrap up everything here as quickly as possible. How about I call you tomorrow night? I should have a better idea of a date for you."

"Yeah, call me tomorrow and we'll talk some more, and Annie?"

"What?"

"I'm glad you answered the phone."

The phone clicked before she could reply. She held the phone to her chest smiling and feeling warm. She began weaving many dreams around Burke and his ranch, hoping that she wouldn't be disappointed.

Over the next couple of days, she found that packing up her apartment was surprisingly easy. All she really needed were her clothes and a few personal items. She looked at her apartment decorated all in black and white. Grinning, she stared at her white couch. It wouldn't last an hour at Burke's place. It was going to be her place too. Her only problem was telling Sonny. She dreaded telling her stepbrother her plans. She had a bad feeling that he wasn't going to be reasonable about her upcoming wedding.

She paced, sat down, and paced again. She had called Sonny earlier, inviting him over to break the news and now, he was due any time. Her hands turned red from all the wringing. The beating of her heart intensified. He was going to be angry but she planned to stand up to him for a change. But, all the waiting had been for nothing. Sonny never showed.

The next day, the confrontation was devastating. Sonny marched into her apartment with his high power business suit and his slicked-back dark hair taking her by surprise.

"You were supposed to be here yesterday."

"I was busy yesterday, but today I came to find out what my little whore of a sister is doing behind my back!" He yelled as he stepped toward her.

"Please, Sonny isn't it time for me to find a life of my own?" she pleaded.

Sonny grabbed her upper arms and shook her. "Your life is what I tell you it is. You got that?"

* * * *

Annie stepped off the plane, sunglasses masking much of her face. She frantically tried to cover the rest with her hair. It was just as she had predicted, Sonny wasn't happy about her plans and he tried to bully her, to threaten her. When that didn't work, he took it out on her with his fists. She got one kick in, and it only enraged him. She could still see the fury in his eyes as he painfully slapped her left cheek, causing her eye to swell. She tried to cover her head, but he punched her in the mouth, making both her nose and lip bleed. When she tried to crawl away from him, he wrapped her hair around his fist and kicked her. Her back and ribs felt incredibly sore. She knew that she was fooling herself hoping that Burke wouldn't notice. The bruises were too fresh and too pronounced. However, she was free. Sonny warned her not to leave and if she was stupid enough to do so, she wasn't to darken his door again. He left her apartment feeling confident that she wasn't going anywhere. Somehow, she got through it. It was over and done and now she had a new life to look forward to.

Annie walked toward the baggage claim and instantly spotted Burke. She had the pleasure of studying him unawares. He still looked so masculine, shoulders were broad and hips lean. He filled out his Wranglers nicely. Handsome wasn't enough to describe him. She took in the sight of him for a moment longer before she approached.

She winced in pain trying to smile. She was so happy to see him, but the look of absolute fury on his face alarmed her. She wanted to back away, but she didn't. She stood her ground waiting for him to say something and was stunned when she found herself enclosed in his strong arms. It was a homecoming for Annie. She was where she belonged.

Burke swore softly.

"Let's get your stuff." Taking her hand, he located her bag, never letting go of her. Leading her out to the truck, he gently helped her in.

Annie could feel his tension; it matched her own. He got into the truck and just sat there looking straight ahead. It had been such a relief when he hadn't asked her any questions in the airport. Emotions were high and she didn't know just how much longer she could hold out without breaking down. It took all she had to stay calm, but she knew that her shaking hands were just the tip of the iceberg. Maybe Burke would wait until they got back to the ranch before questioning her, but she looked at his thunderous expression and knew he wanted answers.

Burke opened his arms and she willingly went into them, snuggling against him. He pulled her tightly against him, rocking her back and forth. That was the end of her struggle to stay strong. Annie put her face against his wide shoulder and cried. It seemed as though once she started, she couldn't stop. She cried not only for the beating she had taken, but also for everything that had gone wrong in her life. She cried for the cruelty of her ex-fiancé and her supposed friend Lisa. She cried for all the loneliness she had suffered when she found that her so-called friends had turned their backs on her. She even cried for the little girl that had lost her mother too early, leaving her in the hands of a nasty stepfather. Finally, she cried in relief that she was in Burke's strong and comforting arms.

Burke ran his hands up and down her back. Eventually, the tears stopped. Slowly, he let her go and gently put her seatbelt on for her and started the truck.

The trip home seemed long, silent, and a bit awkward. She half expected him to turn the truck around and drop her back off at the airport. He didn't ask a beaten weeping woman to be his wife, but to her amazement, he kept going.

Annie tried to smile as Burke helped her down from the truck. She cried out in surprise when he swung her up into his arms and carried her inside. She felt exhausted from her earlier outburst. All she wanted was a hot bath and a warm bed, but she owed Burke some answers, no matter how humiliating they were to her. Burke gently placed her on the threadbare sofa and mumbled that he'd be back with some coffee.

In that moment, Annie wished that she were a beautiful, whole, sexy woman. She wanted to be all those things for Burke, but sadly, she knew the truth. She was a bruised, broken, frigid woman with cuts and bruises on her face and hideous whip marks on her back. Leaning forward she rested her elbows on her knees, groaning in despair as she covered her face with her hands. What if Burke didn't want her anymore? It was so humiliating to allow him to see her this way, but she didn't have a choice, she realized; she didn't have a Plan B.

Annie looked up as Burke entered the room. The look of anger in his eyes was disturbing, and she prayed that his anger was not aimed toward her. She couldn't bear it if it was. She had hoped and dreamed of being his wife and the mother of his children. Now, she had doubts of her dreams ever coming true. She sat up straight, her hands shaking as she took the coffee Burke offered. She watched him sit down in a brown leather chair opposite her. He deserved to know what happened to her, and he deserved the right to back out of their arrangement. Annie's heart twisted while she gazed at his handsome face. It looked so hard and unyielding that it made her fearful of the outcome. Taking a deep breath, she started to explain.

"It was my stepbrother, Sonny," she began, looking at her hands. "He didn't want me to leave New York, and he definitely didn't want me to get married. He slapped me around a bit and he left, warning me to be there when he got back or I'd be sorry. He also told me that if I left, that I was never to darken his door again and that I was cut off financially." Taking a deep breath, Annie clasped her shaking hands together. "As soon as he left I made arrangements with the doorman to have all my boxes shipped here. I packed a bag and got the hell out of there." Annie finally looked up to gage Burke's reaction. She was relieved to see sympathy in his eyes. "I didn't take time to think about how I would look to you when I got here. I would understand if you wanted me to leave." Her eyes silently beseeched him to let her stay.

Burke strode across the wooden floor and took her hand. "We'll get married at the end of the week," he said gruffly. He helped her to stand, then he led her to the brown leather couch. Gently, he sat her down and sat next to her. His arm went around her pulling her toward him, and he kissed her cheek.

Annie finally relaxed and laid her head against his broad shoulder. "I, um... Burke. I'm a virgin and I would like to wait to have sex until after the wedding."

He stiffened against her and she wondered why.

"Something wrong?"

"It's time for bed."

Moments later Burke walked her to her room, her separate room.

Annie gave him a slight smile as he left. She closed the door hoping that everything would turn out all right.

* * * *

Annie awoke to brilliant sunshine and a cool breeze flowing through her window causing her lace curtains to billow. Her momentary confusion melted away to avid delight when she spotted Cat sleeping on her pillow. Annie leaned over and gave her a kiss. She felt buoyant as she realized she was still at the ranch. Burke's tender loving care last night left her with little doubt.

"I can't wait to be Mrs. Burke Dawson!" she told Cat.

Eager to see Burke, she quickly dressed in jeans and a red T-shirt. She grimaced as she looked in the mirror and saw her bruises in all of their colorful glory. Her eye had swelled and her lip was fat. It would take a while for them to heal and fade she realized ruefully. Knowing there was nothing she could do about it, Annie picked up the kitten and headed down the stairs.

The house empty and quiet, very quiet and her disappointment in Burke's absence cut deep. Surely, he would want to greet her on her first morning on the ranch. Annie went out to the front porch hearing the wooden screen door slam shut behind her.

"Now where do you think he is?" she asked Cat.

Shading her eyes with her hand, she looked all around. Burke wasn't in sight. Realizing that she was alone for now, she went back inside for coffee. Despite her disappointment, it thrilled her to be in Texas. Looking around the kitchen as she drank her coffee, Annie realized that she had more than enough to keep her busy until Burke got back. The whole house needed cleaning and the floors were a strange brown color. She just knew it would sparkle and shine with a good scrubbing. Eager to show Burke that she could be an asset to the ranch, she began to do just that.

Hours later she began to rethink her decision to make things sparkle. Her back and arms ached. The place looked good, but she was beat. A quick dinner was all she was able to rustle up.

* * * *

Burke scowled staring at the plate of salad and quiche before him. "What else are you serving?"

"This is it," Annie sat herself opposite of Burke. She smiled at him, happy that he was finally home after such a long day. "Is something wrong?" she asked, noticing the scowl on his face.

"Is this what you eat in New York? I've been working for about fourteen hours. I'm a big man and I need more food than this at dinner."

Annie's happiness quickly deflated. She'd been so eager to please him and had spent most of the day on her hands and knees scrubbing his floors. Not that he'd noticed, obviously. She felt sick to her stomach wondering if she'd fled from one controlling male to another. He'd been so gentle last night, but now his scowl made her apprehensive. She had to make this work since she didn't have a Plan B, or C for that matter. Her doubts quickly waned, however, as she saw just how tired Burke looked. He had washed up when he came in, but his hair and clothes still carried dust and sweat. He was right. He worked hard and expected a big meal.

"You're right," she conceded. "I had no idea you could eat so much. I usually cook just for myself and lately I haven't had much of an appetite. Let me make you a sandwich. I'll know better for tomorrow." She went to the refrigerator and grabbed out the fixings for a sandwich.

Burke's smile surprised her Men and their stomachs.

"Look, I'm a bit grouchy, but I appreciate coming home to a home cooked meal. I usually just heat up a can of something;

Annie gave him a brief nod, and handed him the sandwich. "Good night then. I'm tired."

"You aren't over doing it are you? You still must be in pain."

"I'll take it a bit easier tomorrow, but don't worry, I'll have a hearty meal for you."

Chapter Three

The next few days went by swiftly. The first day at the ranch had set a pattern for both Annie and Burke. He left early in the morning and she didn't see him again until dinner. Annie kept herself busy cleaning the house. It felt a bit lonely, despite Cat's antics, but Annie was glad to be there. The way Burke treated her was her only confusion. He acted quite cold toward her, and he hadn't touched her since the first night. He seemed aloof and she didn't understand why. She could only hope that after they were married and shared a bed he would be a bit more affectionate.

Affection wasn't something Annie had experienced in her life, but she longed for it. It was an ache inside her, to love and to have that love returned. She suspected that she was indeed falling in love with Burke. It was becoming painful hoping for a crumb of approval or a show of feelings from him. She looked forward to the security the marriage would bring her. Surely once they were married, Burke would hold her, kiss her, and whisper sweet loving words to her.

Maybe he didn't find her attractive. It could be that she had read his signals wrong. Lord knew that her past judgment about men was a disaster. She could still hear the echoes of her ex-fiancé laughing at her. She could still hear his taunting voice calling her a cold frigid bitch. Maybe he was right.

Tomorrow was her wedding day, and the thought of displeasing Burke in bed made her anxious. Of course, she had some idea of Burke's expectations. She'd seen movies and read enough romance novels to have some rudimentary knowledge of the act. But in just about all the books she read, love was involved, and Burke didn't love her, might never love her.

Annie was brushing her teeth when she heard the screen door slam. Quickly, she rinsed her mouth and went to see who was in the house. She found Burke rummaging through the refrigerator. He hadn't once come home in the middle of the day before now. It was a nice surprise. Annie watched as he grabbed meat, cheese, and bread and set them on the counter.

"Sit," she insisted. "I'll make you a sandwich." He looked worried and she bit her bottom lip, wondering what was wrong. "What happened to the lunch I made you?"

Burke didn't even look at her. He shrugged his shoulder. "I must have misplaced it somewhere," he replied.

Clearly, something was on his mind. Annie went back to making his lunch, waiting. Waiting for him to call off the wedding, waiting for him to say he didn't want her, waiting for him to say she wasn't worth it. Finally, she couldn't take it anymore. Her nerves felt stretched to the limit. She whirled to face him ready for the blow she knew was coming, maybe not physically, but a blow all the same. "If you don't want to marry me just tell me," she blurted out.

He stood up and walked over to her and he reached for her. He pulled her against him, enfolding her in his arms. Taking a half a step back after a few minutes, he cupped her face in both his hands, lifting her face toward his, looking deeply into her eyes. "We're getting married tomorrow. Nothing changes that, Annie."

Burke lifted her up into his arms. "You look tired." He carried her to bed, putting her down and kissing her forehead. "The house looks great. Take a nap, Annie," he whispered.

* * * *

A hand shaking her shoulder awakened Annie. Her momentary confusion gave way to a loving smile as she realized Burke sat on her bed. "Have I slept long?" The darkening sky out her window answered her question. "Oh no, There's no dinner for you!" she exclaimed in dismay, struggling to get up.

"Slow down, darlin'." Burke held her struggling body tightly against his. "I already ate. I came up earlier, but you looked conked out so I let you sleep. My friend Ted is downstairs and I want you to meet him. I also have some papers we need to sign before the wedding," he explained.

Annie relaxed against him and nodded her head. "I'll be down in a minute," she replied. "I just need to freshen up."

Burke winked at her as he got up. "You look fresh enough for me." He gave her a roguish grin.

Annie felt herself blush as she watched him walk out the room. She just couldn't get enough of his broad shoulders, and she blushed even more when she realized that she'd been staring at his tight rear end. He was such a handsome man, and Annie felt lucky to have him. Quickly she changed into a paisley blue, sleeveless dress and put her wildly curling auburn hair up. Her bruises were still very visible. Experience had taught her that trying to hide them with make up just made them look worse. She whisked on a bit of mascara, dabbed on some lipstick and she was done. She felt a bit nervous looking at her reflection in the mirror. With resignation, Annie turned from the mirror and pulled on a lightweight cardigan to hide the bruises on her arms. Taking a deep breath, she went downstairs.

Burke's friend, Ted, delighted her. He tried to pretend she wasn't black and blue and Annie adored him for it. She liked his whiskey colored eyes and his understanding smile. By the time she had coffee ready for them, Annie felt as though they were on their way to becoming fast friends.

Annie noticed that Burke seemed a bit nervous. She assumed that he was anxious his friend wouldn't find her worthy of him. Annie understood considering he had been married before, and it hadn't worked out. It was amusing that the usually confident Burke Dawson was rattled over something so small.

Her smile quickly faded as Burke handed her papers to sign. "What's this?" she asked quickly scanning the documents.

"I'm not only Burke's friend, but I'm also his lawyer," Ted explained. "He asked me to prepare a prenuptial agreement for the two of you."

Annie knew her eyes were full of accusations. "I don't understand, Burke. Why would we need a prenup? Are you already planning to divorce me?"

"Of course I'm not thinking about divorce, but Annie I was burned once and I couldn't bear to sell any more of my land."

Annie saw the truth in his eyes. She knew what this land meant to him. Glancing down she continued to read, not willing to sign anything until she read it thoroughly. At first, it seemed straightforward, in the event of divorce, he would not give her a settlement, but rather he would pay her alimony as determined by a judge. The next paragraph, however, made her seethe.

"I'm supposed to leave any children we have behind if we divorce?" she asked incredulously. "Are you insane? I could never leave a child of mine behind," she said angrily "I understand about the land. Truly, I do, but as far as children go, you can just forget it. I'm not signing this. I'm sorry." She got up and turned to go to her room. "I'll be out of here tomorrow," she whispered heartbrokenly, and then she ran from the room.

* * * *

Burke watched her retreat in consternation. He knew that he had ambushed her, but he hadn't expected it to go as badly as it did. Shaking his head, he got up and poured himself some whiskey, and quickly downed the first shot. He grabbed another glass and poured two shots. He could see the commiseration in Ted's eyes. They both swigged their shots and slammed the glasses down on the table. Burke wanted to refill his glass, but he knew that he'd had enough. He'd try to make things right with Annie. He had put in too much time and effort to find a wife and he wasn't willing to start from scratch. Besides, he realized that only she would do. "So, counselor, what the hell do I do now?"

"I've got to tell you Buddy, if you give up that little filly upstairs you're crazy. She's as sweet as honey and she's crazy about you."

Burke sighed. "I wouldn't go that far. Sometimes it seems like she barely tolerates me."

"Well, I guess you haven't seen the way she looks at you," Ted insisted. "She's a keeper. If I were you I'd have your lawyer rewrite the prenup and leave the section about children out of it."

Burke was confused. "You are my lawyer."

Ted laughed. "That's why you should heed my advice, old friend."

"Fine," Burke conceded. "Rewrite the damn thing, and in the meantime, I'll try to get her to stay and marry me."

Ted slapped Burke on the shoulder good-naturedly. "Good luck Burke. Just remember groveling is not unmanly." He laughed.

Burke walked him to the door. "You and Sherry will be here for the wedding tomorrow?"

"Wouldn't miss it for the world. It's a good thing you talked the Judge into coming out here. Those bruises Annie's sporting are very visible."

Burke rubbed the back of his neck. "Yeah she's been through the wringer all right. I'm glad Judge Mathers consented to come out here. I didn't want Annie to be embarrassed in town."

Ted shook Burke's hand and headed out. Burke sat down on the front steps looking at the night sky lit in all its splendorous glory contemplating his next move. He just didn't have the energy to look for another wife and he wasn't sure what he'd do if he couldn't get her to change her mind. Maybe he was being an ass. Maybe he should just admit to himself that he wanted Annie for Annie and not as an unpaid housekeeper. When he had first started his wife search he had naively thought that almost any woman would do, but now he realized that he needed Annie.

Burke looked up at the sky again asking God what he should say to her to make things right again. He felt so hopeless and out of his element. Hell, what did he know about women? Obviously not enough to keep the women in his house happy, that much he knew. A shooting star appeared and traversed the sky, leaving Burke more hopeful than he'd been in a long time.

* * * *

Annie threw her clothes haphazardly into her suitcase, but she didn't care. She could hardly see as tears blurred her vision. How she'd ever gotten herself into such a mess she would never know. Her heart beat out of her chest. Where would she go? Finally, she decided that it didn't matter. Anywhere else was fine. She had some money in the bank and if she was frugal and found a job, she'd be fine.

Sitting on the bed, she blew her nose. A ghost of a smile spread across her face as she watched Cat jumping in and out of her suitcase. She had to get herself together. If she looked inside, she knew she would find the strength to go on. Shakily, she wiped away the last of her tears and went to the window, looking at the ranch she'd fallen in love with. There were a few of the horses romping in the corral and she smiled. She liked Texas and she liked small towns. There had to be a lot to pick from in Texas. All she had to do was to find one. She could buy a cheap car and just drive, this time taking her time to make a decision. Annie felt a bit better knowing that she had a plan. Her heart was still shattered, but she'd get over it, she hoped.

She took a deep unsteady breath. Turning from the window, she jumped, seeing Burke leaning against the doorframe watching her. Regret and pain were evident in his blue eyes and she knew that her eyes mirrored his. Annie quickly looked away. She didn't want him to sway her into signing her future babies away. It was inconceivable to her that he could even have thought she'd go along with his grand plan. She steeled herself and stood up straighter. There was no way she was going to let him come into her room and call her darlin' and make her change her mind. No way in hell.

"I heard you crying and I'm as sorry as I can be, Annie. I never want to be the cause of your pain. He stepped into the room until he stood right in front of her. "Well, Miss Douglas, you give one hell of a fight." He ran his finger through his hair. "I really thought I was right in this situation." He sighed heavily. "Annie, I'm sorry, I should have talked to you about the prenuptial agreement. I realize now that it must have seemed like I ambushed you."

"Damn right it did!" Annie put her hands on her hips, giving him her most defiant look.

Burke took her hands in his, running his calloused thumbs over the top of her smooth ones, caressing her. "I made a mistake and I don't want to lose you. I told Ted to rewrite the prenup, omitting the part about the children."

The contrast between their hands was huge. Hers were so small and white and his were deeply tanned and rough. She felt a quickening inside as he continued to rub her hands. She felt so much for this man and she wanted to marry him. His mere touch made her tingle in places she never knew could tingle and it made it hard for her to think. Pulling her hands away, she walked over to the window. She felt him right behind her, near enough that she could feel the heat of him, but he wasn't touching her.

"I'm glad you had him rewrite it," she told him after a lengthy silence. "I understand about the land, really I do," she continued, as she turned around into his embrace. "I want this to work between us. It hurts though that you would even think that I would have signed that despicable piece of paper. Maybe we don't know each other well enough to marry. Maybe we should wait awhile," she said pensively.

"No," Burke insisted. "It's obvious that you have doubts." He wrapped his arms around her and placed his chin on her head. "A lot of it has to do with my ex-wife."

"You never talk about her," Annie accused, taking a step back. She had to crane her neck to see his blue eyes. They looked troubled. "But sometimes I think she's still here between us."

* * * *

Burke sighed. He didn't like talking about that woman, but now he didn't have a choice. "Let's go downstairs and sit in front of the fire and I'll tell you the grisly tale."

Taking her hand, he led her downstairs to the comfortable couch in front of the massive stone fireplace. They sat side by side staring into the leaping yellow and orange flames.

He took a deep breath. It was difficult to talk about his ex. He didn't want to dredge up all the painful memories, but Annie deserved to know. He didn't want secrets between them. He continued to stare into the fire as he told his story.

"I met her at a stock show in Fort Worth. I was showing my prize bull and had won a big prize purse. I was elated and I wanted to celebrate so I went to the White Elephant Saloon for a few drinks with a couple friends of mine and there she was. Even now, I realize what a fool I was, allowing her beauty to sway me and she was a beauty! She latched on to me, batting her eyelashes at me, pressing her breasts against my arm at any opportunity. I felt honored that she picked me. We ended up in bed that night and wanting to impress her, I took her to a very expensive hotel. She assumed that I was a rich cattleman, especially since I won that prize purse. I never in my dreams imagined that I could land a girl like her. I was living all alone at the ranch and thought what the hell, why not get married? We got married the next day."

Burke got up and put another log on the fire. He didn't look at Annie. He didn't want to see her disgust. He didn't speak for a while and neither did she. Finally, he sat back down and continued.

"I didn't know that she thought I was rich. My ranch was doing well, and I put any spare money back into the land hoping to be rich one day. I neglected the house and never bothered to update it. You could imagine what she thought as we drove up to it for the first time. That's when I realized that she was a shrew. She accused me of tricking her into marriage and told me that she couldn't believe that she had married 'a struggling old cowboy with a patch of land.' The woman I thought was beauty, kindness, and full of sunshine was really an ugly spoiled brat. I wasn't poor by any means, but that wasn't good enough for Alice and I ended up spending money, earmarked for the ranch, on her to make her happy, but it was never enough. It was a stupid thing to do financially. In these times with the price of beef uncertain and property taxes going up, I shouldn't have dipped into my savings.

"Finally, I told her that the money tree had dried up. She was spitting mad and just like that she left. A couple weeks later, her lawyer insisted on half of all assets in a divorce settlement. I tried to fight her, but by then she had found herself a new sucker to pay her way. I had to give her half my land and I sold half my cattle. I'm lucky I still have a house to live in."

Annie snuggled up against Burke, surprising him. He half expected her to go to her room and continue packing.

She put her arms around him, giving him a big hug. "I'm sorry you went through such an awful time."

Burke put his arms around her drawing her closer. He didn't know what good deed he'd done to deserve Annie, but he wasn't about to question it. "I want this marriage to be a partnership. I want us to help each other to rebuild this ranch and to build a future for both our children and us. I'm so sorry I made you cry earlier. It tore my heart out to know I was the cause of your misery." He put his hand under her chin and lifted her face toward him. "Forgive me?"

She nodded as Burke swooped down to kiss her. He kissed her gently, coaxingly, nibbling at her bottom lip. She made small cries of delight. He licked the seam between her lips and she opened up for him. Soon she was matching her tongue to his. Annie put her arms around his neck pulling his mouth against hers even harder.

Eventually he broke off the kiss, and lifted her to put her on his lap, holding her close. "Good God, Annie if we don't stop we'll never have a proper wedding night."

Closing her eyes, she laid her head on Burke's shoulder and snuggled against him.

He could feel her finally relaxing in his arms, but her squirming was driving him to the brink of madness. Tomorrow was his wedding day and he prayed that he was making the right decision. It was a leap of faith, and lately his faith had really waned, but looking down at Annie as she slept, his heart lurched. He wanted to take this leap of faith. Maybe Ted was right and she was a keeper.

He really hoped so as he carried her up to her bed, put her under the covers, and kissed her tenderly on the forehead. She looked so peaceful, so lovely and he hoped that he never brought her misery again.

He could kick himself for bringing her any type of pain. That little gal had been through enough. He gazed at her bruises and her fat lip. It must have hurt when they kissed. Why didn't she say anything? He wondered if her beating had been one of many. Brave, that's what she was. His very own green-eyed warrior who threw caution to the wind and came to Texas to marry him.

She would have a good life here. They would have babies and the ranch would prosper. A scowl crossed his face. He couldn't afford to dream. He did that once and look where it had gotten him. All he could really hope for was friendship. He'd give her children they both wanted them, but emotions couldn't play into this arrangement. It would be more a business deal, a type of partnership. That's how it had to be.

Chapter Four

Annie sat up in her bed. The sun streamed through her window bringing warmth and a good measure of happiness. This was her wedding day. She shot out of bed and hugged herself. She wanted to get up on her bed and jump up and down, something that she had never been allowed to do in the past, but she was afraid that Burke might hear her down in the kitchen.

Burke... she pressed her fingertips to her lips remembering their kisses from the night before. He had made her feel beautiful, even womanly and she wanted to open her window and shout her happiness to the world.

"It's my big day Cat! I'm going to be a wife and I'm going to have a family. Maybe dreams do come true."

Cat just stared at her.

Quickly, she dressed, wanting to spend her wedding day breakfast with Burke.

She wasn't quite sure how she should greet him. Should she go right up to him and kiss him? He might not like that. Sometimes he could be so cold and aloof. She couldn't wait to get married; she knew that things would be so different. They would labor side by side working the ranch and affection between them would be natural. Annie finally decided that a bright smile would be just the right greeting for her groom and she went downstairs.

Annie's smile quickly dissipated. Once again, Burke was not there to have breakfast with her. Trying to be optimistic, she reasoned that he was probably just out in the barn tending to the animals. The animals wouldn't stop needing tending just because it was their wedding. A special breakfast was just what he needed when he came in. Annie found a Belgium waffle maker in the cupboard the other day and today she planned to make use of it.

She made coffee and mixed the waffle batter, humming all the while, excited to see Burke. He had come to mean so much to her so quickly, and she was both pleased and a bit frightened. She hoped that he was really what he seemed, a man of integrity, gentleness, and honesty. The waffle maker finally heated and she began making waffles.

She began to get impatient as she used the last of the batter. Looking at the plate piled high with golden brown waffles, she felt pleased with her accomplishment. Surely, this was enough breakfast for any man, but where was he? She even put out Cat's food while she waited.

Finally, she walked out to the barn to find him. She put on her best smile and entered, but to her dismay, he wasn't there. Annie's heart began to beat harder. Did he leave? He could have at least told her that the wedding had been canceled. If he thought she was going to just leave, he was crazy. They had a deal.

Burke rounded the corner and nearly knocked her over. He quickly held on to her waist to keep her from falling. He smiled at her but she didn't smile back. "What's wrong?"

"You tell me."

"Annie I don't have time for games. Just tell me what's got you so riled."

"Riled?" Annie stepped away from him, put her hands on her hips, and shook her head. "Riled?"

"Well isn't that what they call it when a woman is all mad about nothing? Wait I take it back. What did I do?"

She couldn't figure him out. "Now you ask what you did? What happened to riled?"

"I've been married before and I know that look. We really don't have time for this."

Taking a deep breath, she studied his face. He really did look as though he had no idea why she was upset. Slowly she let out her breath and gave him a weak smile. "When I couldn't find you, I thought you decided to call off the wedding."

"Never gave it a thought. You can't just jump to conclusions."

"I can't get all *riled up*?"

"They don't say that in New York?"

"Not to a woman and expecting to live."

Burke laughed deep and loud. "You sure are something."

Grabbing Burke's hand, she pulled him back toward the house and into the kitchen. "We have waffles to eat."

Burke dutifully sat at the kitchen table and ate more than his share of the waffles. He watched her intently during the meal, eventually satisfied that she was all right. "Oh hell!" He looked at his watch. "We're getting married in a few hours."

Annie's eyes grew wide, "I have to get ready and the kitchen is a mess and..."

Burke took control. He stood and grabbed her hand. He leaned down and gave her a quick kiss. "Up into the shower with you, I'll tidy the kitchen."

Annie nodded and started up the stairs.

"Don't use all the hot water; I still have to shower too!" Burke called out to her.

* * * *

Annie felt grateful that Burke was considerate enough to have the wedding at the ranch. She still had bruises on her face and had no desire to go to town. She smiled at her reflection in the mirror. She loved her dress. It was a strapless white silk creation with a lace overlay. The lace was in the pattern of roses and Annie just loved it. It was the most daring dress she'd ever worn. When she bought it in New York, she hadn't anticipated the bruises on her arms, but she pretended now that they weren't there. She left her curly auburn hair loose, falling down her back, except for the right side, which she swept up with a pearl encrusted comb. She put on her pearl necklace and earrings that were the only legacy she had from her mother. She didn't spare a moment of thought for the woman who never seemed to want her. The array of emotion caught her off guard. She felt buoyant, nervous, lucky, and even more nervous. Leaving her own room, she hoped for the last time, she joined her groom downstairs.

Annie's eyes misted as she took in the sight before her. A lot had been done in the last few hours. The family room had been totally transformed. There were red roses everywhere; someone had erected an arch in front of the grand fireplace, draped in red roses. Looking down, she saw the white runner that would lead her to her future husband. A woman she assumed to be Ted's wife, Sherry handed her a bouquet of yellow roses. Annie smiled her thanks.

She couldn't help but notice that they were the same flowers that she had fallen in love with, both at the old cabin and at this very house. The whole room smelled like roses, heavenly roses. It definitely made her feel like this was all a long-awaited homecoming.

Annie looked straight ahead and caught Burke's gaze. She read the approval in his eyes and she knew that he didn't find her lacking. Drawing her courage from him, she proceeded down the aisle. Her smile grew shaky as she took his hand, and she felt like her heart would burst. Burke looked so handsome in his black suit and she could tell that it was expensive and tailor-made. He looked striking. and she felt proud to be standing next to him. She became so lost in him that she barely made the right responses to the judge. She smiled when Burke took out not one but two rings for them to exchange. Annie hadn't given it much thought, but it delighted her that he intended to wear a wedding ring.

Judge Mathers finally pronounced them Man and Wife and told Burke that he could kiss the bride.

* * * *

Kiss her? Burke wanted to eat her. God she looked so beautiful. Her dress molded to all her delectable curves, driving him crazy. He looked into her misted eyes and winked at her as he moved his lips closer to hers. He wrapped his arms around her and gave her a searing kiss of possession. They became so lost in each other at that moment that they almost forgot about their guests. Burke heard someone clear his or her throat and reluctantly released Annie.

Joyously, Annie greeted and hugged their guests. It already looked as though she and Sherry would be fast friends, and the Judge was so rollie pollie that he could barely hug her. Ted came and gave her a quick hug and kiss on the cheek. Burke felt lucky to have her at his side. He was proud of how nice and friendly she acted toward all his friends.

Burke opened a bottle of champagne with a loud popping of the cork. The sparkling libation bubbled up and out of the bottle. "Quick, get the glasses!" He cried, in amusement. He poured six glasses and handed them out. The last one went to, Mrs. Harvy a slender older woman with an unmistakable twinkle in her eye. She had just put a beautiful wedding cake on the table and accepted the glass. "About time you found yourself the right filly," she remarked with a mischievous smile.

"I'm glad you approve." He kissed her on the cheek, then walked her over to his bride and made the introductions. "Annie, honey this wonderful woman is not only a friend, but she is the best cook in all of Weltworth."

Mrs. Harvy blushed at his compliment. She took Annie's hand and simply said, "She'll do."

With that, everyone drank a toast to the newlyweds. Annie seemed to be having great time getting to know everyone especially Sherry.

Soon enough the champagne was gone and every one had eaten some cake. He hoped that the guests would leave soon so he could get some alone time with his bride, but just as Ted was about to go, Annie turned to Burke and asked about the prenup. "I'd really like to sign it if it's been rewritten," she said softly.

Burke looked into her eyes trying to gage her reaction. He wanted her to want to sign it. He'd thought about it a lot last night and decided that he really wanted *her* more. He'd thought to give it a bit of time and then have her sign a document relinquishing any claim she might have on the land. Now, she had made it a lot easier.

"Ted," he called out.

Ted turned as he was unlocking the car door. "What do you need?"

"Bring the papers we'll sign them now."

Ted grabbed his briefcase.

He handed the papers first to Annie for her perusal. She gave Burke a smile and signed. Burke signed too and handed them back to his friend. "Well, what are you waiting around for?" he teased Ted. "I have some honeymooning to do."

Ted just grinned. "Well, you two have at it," he teased back. "Remember Burke old boy, slow and steady wins the race."

Annie gasped and Burke threw his head back and laughed.

After Ted and his wife left, they were finally alone. He turned to Annie and embraced her, loving the feel of her against his hard body. Her dress impressed him, but he wanted her out of it. He lifted her into his arms and he could see by Annie's wide eyes that she was surprised. He took the steps two at a time carrying her into his room.

Burke watched the display of emotions as they played across her face. He saw fear and determination. He hoped to God that he could make it good for her. He smiled to himself as he remembered Ted's advice. Slow and steady would probably be the right thing to do.

Burke set her down on her feet and turned her toward him. He looked into her eyes cupping her shoulders with his big hands. Caressing her creamy white shoulders he felt her begin to tremble and he hoped to hell it was out of desire and not out of fear. He knew that she must be somewhat nervous; what virgin wouldn't be? Running his hands up and down her arms, he felt her skin begin to warm. She trembled again. "Cold?" he asked.

Annie blushed and looked at his chest. "I don't know what to do."

"Do what you want to."

Annie put her arms around Burke's neck and pulled his head towards hers for a kiss.

The kiss started soft and gentle. Burke tried to rein himself in, not wanting to scare his new bride, but to his surprise and pleasure, Annie deepened the kiss and put her tongue in his mouth. He could feel her smile as their tongues danced together. Burke pulled her tight against him and could feel her nipples grow hard through the fabric of her dress. His hands began to work quickly, unbuttoning her gown, but much to his dismay, the buttons were so tiny that he needed to see them to unbutton them.

He quickly turned her around and unbuttoned her gown. He was tempted to rip it off, but he knew how a woman treasured her wedding gown and it would do nothing to calm her nerves. He finally unbuttoned her gown down her back, but her hands held up the front of her dress refusing to let it drop. Burke took a deep breath as he remembered that he needed patience.

She turned to him, her face flushed with desire. "Maybe if you took off some of your clothes first..."she suggested shyly.

Burke grinned. At first, he was half-afraid she was going to suggest that they consummate their marriage another time, but that he could do. He began to unbutton his dress shirt, actually feeling a bit self-conscious at her rapt attention. She gasped as his chest came into view. He knew that he didn't have an ounce of fat on him, with all the physical work he did, but he never made a woman gasp before. He liked it.

There was something wrong with her breathing as she stared at him. She actually panted.

Burke felt incredible by her reaction to him. He couldn't wait to see her. He cocked his eyebrow as he looked at her and she blushed. She knew that it was her turn to undress. He could tell she was nervous, but he could also see the desire in her glorious green eyes. He watched as she turned around and let her gown drop. Burke stared in fascination as he looked at her back, but he began to frown as his perusal went downward. Annie had whip marks on the small of her back, her buttocks, and the top of her thighs. He suddenly felt sick. How could anyone mark such perfection? He wasn't sure what to do; he wanted to kill someone, but instead, he simply walked toward her and turned her to face him.

She looked so very beautiful. Her breasts were full and her hard pink nipples ripe for the tasting. Her stomach was flat and sexy and she was nicely curved in all the right places. He looked lower and her auburn curls excited him. Pulling her toward him, he kissed her as his hands roamed her bare back, careful not to touch her scars. He didn't want to address them just yet. His only goal now was to make Annie feel like a woman, his woman.

He held her with one arm and shimmied out of his boxers with the other. His hard arousal pressed against her stomach.

Annie looked down, turned white and backed away. "Surely that won't... I mean we couldn't possibly... you wouldn't," she stammered.

Burke laughed lightly and pulled her back into his embrace. "Don't worry we'll be a great fit. I don't want you frightened, but believe me darlin', it's not as bad as it looks."

Annie looked doubtful, but they continued to kiss and explore each other. She touched his hard stomach, avoiding his erection and then rubbed his back. Finally, she began to relax and she even laughed as Burke lifted her in his arms and gently laid her on the bed.

He watched her for a moment, noticing the glow of her skin and he wanted her more than he could ever remember wanting any other woman. He took a deep breath, reminding himself to take it slow. Annie opened her arms to him and he accepted the invitation, kissing her rosy breasts, making her cry out in ecstasy. When he suckled her hard nipples, she practically sprang up from the bed. Slowly he kissed his way down to her stomach, hands stroked her inner thighs, making her wet.

Slowly he entered her, feeling just how tight and slick she was. She bucked as though she wanted more of him. He seemed to be going too slow for her. Burke continued to stoke her as he entered her. She was like a wild animal when she finally spun out of control and yelled her passion. Burke thrust into her as she slowed, and he felt her stiffen in pain. Tears spilled from her eyes.

He tenderly kissed away her tears and murmured encouragement to her. Soon enough he felt her move against him again. He kissed her as he thrust in and out of her. He could feel her moving against him, matching him stroke for stroke. He wouldn't be able to last much longer. Suddenly he felt her contract wildly around him, squeezing him as she came. Thrusting two more times, he flung his head back as he spilled himself into her.

Burke stilled inside her, enjoying the feel of her around him. She brought him a sense of peace he hadn't known since before he met his ex-wife. He luxuriated in the serenity as he kissed her face and neck. Slowly he withdrew and rolled off her, bringing her with him and splaying her on top of him. He held her as he gazed into her eyes. In her sleepy eyes he could see her passion and satisfaction, and he smiled as she snuggled against his side, her head on his shoulder and her arm on his chest.

The tenderness he felt for her overwhelmed him and for a moment, he wanted to run. He hadn't bargained for this, he hadn't bargained for Annie. This was just sex and nothing else; he couldn't afford emotional tangles again, especially not with Annie. She could wield the power to devastate him if he allowed it. He vowed to enjoy her but never love her. He would give her kindness, sex, and hopefully children. That would be enough. It would have to be.

Chapter Five

Annie woke up feeling like a budding rose that had finally opened. She felt very sexy and much loved. She wasn't used to this warm and fuzzy feeling, but she relished in it. Her one disappointment was that Burke was not in bed with her when she woke, but she knew that the ranch came first. She smiled to herself; she was now a rancher's wife. Scooping up Cat, she nuzzled her under her chin. Getting out of bed, naked, she went to the window, and greeted the sun as an old friend. Feeling as radiant as the sunrays, she wanted to dance. Grabbing her robe, she held it to her like a dance partner, waltzing around the room, laughing the whole time. Joy was hers for the taking and she was taking it. When she noticed Burke watching her from the door she came to a sudden stop giving him a brilliant smile. Walking toward him, she tried to embrace him, he only half-heartedly hugged her in return. She saw regret in his eyes and wondered what was wrong, but before she could ask, Burke mumbled something about the day wasting away and he left.

All of Annie's joy and sunshine faded in that moment. She had been on the cusp of a brand new wonderful life and Burke somehow snatched it away. Dejected, she sat on the bed wondering what had gone wrong. She had thought that the previous night had been magical, but then again she had nothing to compare it to. All of her doubts and insecurities were coming back to haunt her. Tears began to fall down her face. Angrily she dashed them away and got up. She had a spine, a backbone and she wasn't going to let him ruin her day.

Annie felt better for making a strong stand and got herself dressed. She'd go through her day as though nothing bothered her, but deep inside her heart was breaking. She swore herself for a fool, imagining herself dancing naked around the room. Nobody ever loved her and maybe nobody ever would, but she had a wonderful place to live and she had hope for children. That would have to be enough.

The days were beginning to get warmer. Annie skipped breakfast and decided to work in the vegetable garden. It was her garden now and she felt a sense of pride as she looked at it. She wasn't exactly sure what was what, but everything was planted in neat rows. It obviously needed tending and Annie grabbed some gloves and proceeded to weed it, laughing often at Cat's romping and exploring. She had been at it for about three hours when Burke rode in. Shielding her eyes from the sun, she watched him. God, he looked so masculine and she felt her body responding to him. Her nipples tightened as he drew near.

Annie stood up too fast and swayed a bit, feeling dizzy.

I've probably stayed out in the sun too long, she mused.

"You'll need to wear a hat out here," Burke admonished her. He gave her a long look and locked on her chest He gave her a roguish look and almost laughed as she blushed. "What's for lunch?"

"I'm sorry, I wanted to finish weeding, and I forgot the time," she explained.

Burke looked at her sunburned skin. "Don't you wear sunblock in the city?"

"I couldn't find any."

He looked over the garden and she could see his face grow irritated. "Don't tell me, you've never gardened before. You've pulled up more plants than weeds," he sighed.

"All I can do is apologize, Burke. I do have a lot to learn." She turned away from him and started toward the house with a frown. She suddenly stopped and whirled on him. "You know I've been bullied and hurt by every man in my life! Hell even my mother didn't love me. Somehow, I thought you were different. I should have stuck to what I know: men can't be trusted and they just hurt you in the end!"

She thought she saw a look of regret in Burke's eyes before he turned and walked toward his horse. Sadly, she watched him ride away, feeling as though all her hopes and dreams were riding away with him. She stood there until she could no longer see him.

Her head ached and she started to feel the pain of her sunburn. Slowly she went in the house and took an aspirin for both her head and burn. Next, she found a bottle of aloe and slathered it all over her red-burnt skin. It soothed the outside of her, but there was no soothing her broken heart.

Maybe she should have known better. She had seen his temper on occasions, but somehow she dismissed it. How could he be so kind and gentle one minute and so irritated another? Annie supposed that was just the way of men.

It hurt to move, her shoulders, arms and face were on fire. It was a good thing she wore jeans or she wouldn't be able to walk. Annie went into the family room and sat on the worn sofa. She could still feel the house embracing her, welcoming her, inviting her to make it her home. Sadly, she didn't know if she could accept such an invitation. She wondered about all the Dawson women before her and if they had such hard men to live with. A strong breeze came through the front window bringing the fresh scent of the red and yellow roses with it. Somehow, that brought her comfort. She knew she was strong enough to fight for what she wanted. The problem was that she wasn't sure what she wanted anymore.

Gingerly she got up and went into the kitchen, made a simple stew and set it on low to simmer. She set Cat's food on the floor and took a moment to watch her eat. For such a little thing, she sure ate a lot. Slowly, she made her way upstairs and climbed into bed, their bed, and promptly fell asleep.

A few hours later, Annie awoke crying out in pain. She sat up in the darkness and wondered how long she'd been sleeping. At least she'd learned her lesson about the hot Texas sun. She got out of bed making the least possible movements and gingerly went downstairs. She was hungry, and she needed more aloe. Aloe first, she decided, definitely aloe first. Walking into the kitchen, she noticed the dirty dish in the sink. He'd come home after all. Annie tried to tell herself to buck up, that it didn't matter what he did. Nevertheless, deep inside her, she was both glad and very nervous. She knew she wasn't in any condition to spar with him tonight.

She grabbed the bottle of aloe and jumped when she felt Burke's big hand take it from her. She turned in surprise ready to face him down. The look of concern on his face surprised her. He took her small hand in his and led her to the family room. Without a word, he sat her down and removed her shirt. She had taken her bra off earlier because the straps irritated her burn. Slowly he covered her arms and shoulders with the aloe. He even got the back of her neck and part of her back that she couldn't reach earlier. His touch was tender, not sexual in any way. Annie had a hard time trying to reconcile this Burke with the one who had been so annoyed earlier over a little mistake. She was glad for the truce though.

They sat in silence. What was there to say? She'd already apologized about the garden and she'd be damned if she would again. He needed to be more understanding. Didn't he know that this was all new to her? Couldn't he see that she was trying? Hell, he never even mentioned how good the house looked or how much the floors shone.

Same story, different locale. She'd wasted her efforts once again. It would be so much easier if she didn't feel so attracted to him.

"Darlin' you're going to be in a world of hurt in the next few days," he commiserated.

Annie took a deep breath and turned her head to look at him. "I already am," she said, with a halfhearted smile.

"If you weren't in pain I'd take you in my arms and hold you. I'm sorry about earlier. You don't deserve my anger. In fact now that I think about it, it's actually kind of funny that you don't know a weed from a plant," he said sincerely.

Annie groaned. "I was just trying to show you what a wonderful wife you married and I failed miserably."

Burke kissed the top of her head. "As soon as I can touch you without hurting you I'll show you just how little of a failure you are."

Annie looked puzzled. "What do you mean?"

Burke laughed at her confusion. "Honey, last night was the best in my life. We are as explosive in bed as we seem to be out of it. I'm determined to keep the fireworks in the bedroom from now on."

"So last night was good?"

"Why, you didn't think so? I thought you enjoyed it, Annie."

Annie looked away. "I thought it was fine."

"Fine? What's that supposed to mean? I thought it was better than fine."

She studied him. "Are you being honest? I was good? I need you to be honest. I know it was my first time and I didn't know what to do, yet again."

Burke carefully kissed her cheek. "I said it was the best and I meant it."

Annie relaxed. A glow emanated from her at his praise. It made her ecstatic to know that she had brought him as much pleasure as he had brought her. It made her wish for a brief moment that she could shove Burke's words down Jeffrey's throat. She wondered why she even thought of that creep anymore, but his words had really shattered her. Now she knew he could never hurt her again. She was a passionate pleasing woman who enjoyed sleeping with her husband.

That night when they went to bed neither touched each other. Annie knew that Burke was afraid to hurt her sunburn and she was glad for his consideration. Even Cat slept at the bottom of the bed instead of on Annie's pillow. Once again she woke to an empty bed, but she realized that she was either going to have to accept it or get up earlier. She decided that she would have find out how much earlier.

Burke laughed as she approached him on the subject that night at dinner. "I get up with the roosters, darlin'. I'm perfectly fine in the morning. You already pack a great lunch for me to take every day and the dinners have been delicious."

He took a good long look at her. "Do you want me to wake you when I get up?" he asked.

"It's a lonely feeling to wake up alone."

Burke laughed and gave her a roughish grin. "But the nights are anything but lonely."

Annie felt her face turn red. "I know. Well, lately I don't know, but I'm hopeful for when my sunburn fades."

Burke threw his head back, laughed and gave her a wolfish grin. "Oh, darlin' we'll be making up for lost time, believe me."

Annie was both embarrassed and excited by her husband's teasing. She'd always heard of a man's needs and frankly, she was shocked to realize that she had needs too. Now that Burke had awakened her sexually she felt as though he'd created a monster. Maybe it was the fact that they couldn't that made her want it even more. She didn't know, but wanting him preoccupied her mind a great bit over the next few days.

Finally, her burn and bruises disappeared. Annie studied her image in the mirror critically, but she had to admit she'd never looked better. She hoped that Burke agreed because she had wifely plans for him tonight. Annie put on her yellow sundress. The one she had first worn to the ranch.

She went downstairs. There really wasn't much to do. Dinner was cooking and she had worked hard cleaning earlier. Cat napped in the sun. She decided to go out to the barn and meet the horses. She had wanted to get a look at them. The red barn was the most well-kept building on the ranch. The smell was a bit overwhelming, but she figured she'd get used to it. She stopped at the first stall and looked in. The head of chestnut colored horse appearing right in front of her startled her. She gasped, taking a step back and then smiled at the horse. "I live here now," she told him. "I would like for us to be friends." She took a cautious step forward. She wanted to touch it, but she knew she was out of her element and didn't want to explain a bitten hand to Burke. "My name is Annie," she continued until she heard a slight snicker.

* * * *

Burke walked into the barn. He grew enchanted while he watched Annie talking to his roan. She'd actually introduced herself and he wanted to double over in laughter, but didn't want to offend her. God, she was beautiful. Best of all, she looked fully healed. He could feel himself getting hard as his eyes devoured her.

Annie turned and smiled brilliantly, lighting up the whole barn. "Well, hello, cowboy." She moved toward him, swaying her hips, stopping right in front of him, locking her green eyes with his. He could read the blatant desire there.

Burke pulled her against him. He buried his hands in her long auburn hair enjoying the softness of it. He brought her closer and dipped his head to kiss her. He nipped at her lips giving her light, teasing kisses. Raining her face and neck in sumptuous kisses, he paid particular attention to the place between her neck and shoulder. He felt her shiver. Her eagerness seemed to match his.

He drew back, gazed into her heavy lidded eyes, and saw her look of desire. It felt as though it could explode at any moment. He grabbed her hand and a blanket, and led her to a couple of stacked hay bales. They looked to be the perfect height for what he planned.

Burke covered the bales with the blanket and bent Annie over them. He reached up her skirt, ripped off her panties and pushed her dress up over her back. Burke admired her perfectly rounded rear end for a moment before he untied the halter on her sundress, allowing her large breasts to fall heavily toward the ground. Peppering the back of her neck with kisses, he rolled both nipples between his fingers. He heard her moan and felt her hips begin to move. He knew what she wanted, what he wanted. He let go of her breasts and reached around her waist as he massaged her. Quickly he guided himself inside her and thrust for all he was worth. Nothing in his life compared to the feeling he experienced as he made love to her. Burke felt her tense as she came all around him bringing him to an immediate completion, and what a completion it was. He'd never had completion quite like that in his life. He was spent as he held onto Annie after they both finished. Finally, he pulled away, adjusted his jeans, and lifted her up into his arms. He sat on the bales of hay with her on his lap. The look she gave him was one of amazement and satisfaction. He couldn't help feeling proud to have brought those expressions to her face.

* * * *

Annie reached up and stroked Burke's face, loving the way it felt, whiskers and all. The back of her neck was probably rubbed red from all his kisses, but she didn't care. She tried so hard to get her breathing under control, but her heart still raced as she snuggled against Burke's chest. That had been definitely worth the wait. She never dreamed of feeling so good. It was pleasure beyond anything she'd ever felt and she didn't want to talk or move. She wanted this feeling of joy to last as long as possible. You could never predict tomorrow, so she was set on embracing this day.

She spotted her torn panties on the hard dirt, and suddenly felt dirty and sexy simultaneously. Slowly, she released herself from

Burke's hold retied her halter-top and reached for her panties. She wadded them up in her hand and gave Burke a sideways look before she scampered to the house. She could hear Burke's laughter all the way to the porch.

The leach, he hadn't even taken off any off his clothes. It seemed improper, but hell, it felt wonderful. Annie smiled realizing just how wild she made Burke. It was definitely good for her self-esteem. She grew giddy just thinking about it.

She skipped halfway up the stairs and stopped.

Imagine Annie Douglas—make that Annie Dawson— skipping.

She ran the rest of the way up and flopped down on her bed. She never wanted to feel any other feelings but joy and satisfaction, and naughtiness she had to admit, for the rest of her life.

Suddenly, Burke jumped on the bed beside her and she squealed in delight. He gave her a quick kiss. Lifting himself up on one elbow, he gazed at her face. He gently brushed the hair from her face and kissed her again. "Let's go out and celebrate," he suggested.

Annie kissed him back, long and lovingly. "Can we afford to go out?"

"Your concern makes me proud." He cupped her face in his hands and kissed her eyelids. He pulled away and smiled. "I think we can afford the diner," he teased, "as long as you don't order extra fries."

* * * *

They held hands as they entered the diner. Noreen looked delighted to see them and readily came out from behind the counter, her graying hair falling from her bun a bit at a time. She quickly took Annie's hand. "She's got that special glow about her," she teased, her eyes full of mischief. "What do you think Old Rowdy?" She motioned to the counter. "Doesn't she look just like a newlywed should?"

Annie blushed at all the attention. The whole diner looked at them. She heard Old Rowdy mumble something she couldn't make out, but it didn't seem to matter as Noreen continued to chatter and lead them to their table.

Noreen seated them and announced to the whole diner that she had set them up together and was wholly responsible for their happy marriage. She preened as the other customers applauded, and turned back to the couple smiling. "Now tell me the truth," she started, "he's treating you okay isn't he? I'd hate to have to lay him out on the ground for meanness." She laughed, her eyes sparkling.

Burke looked put out, but Annie laughed good-naturedly. "He's a nice man Noreen. I have no cause for complaint."

"Well, of course he's nice, I wouldn't have fixed you up with just any yahoo."

Old Rowdy, Hank, and Bo were starting to make noises at the counter. They needed refills on their coffee. "Hold on you, old farts," she yelled to them. "Can't you see that I'm busy?" She left muttering under her breath.

Annie was glad she wasn't one of the old farts. Noreen didn't look happy with them. She couldn't hear what she said, but it was obviously a scolding. She looked at Burke and they both laughed. "I just love her."

Burke held her hand on the table caressing it. "She is a character," he agreed.

Annie almost fell on the floor laughing when Noreen came back without asking them what they wanted and placed burgers and fries before them. Noreen's smile was so bright that Annie didn't have the heart to say anything.

Burke seemed to take it in stride. He did laugh though as he heard the next table grumble that those must be their burgers they'd been waiting forever for.

They both ate with gusto, having worked up an appetite earlier in the barn. They were just finishing when Burke excused himself.

Annie sat there happily, waiting for Burke to return. Unfortunately, she could hear the conversation at the next table. She didn't turn to see who sat there.

"She's certainly not as pretty as Alice," The first woman said.

"You're right. Why she has no sex appeal at all. What was Burke thinking to marry such a dowdy little thing?" The second woman said.

"Obviously he married her to get back the land that her brother bought. He probably did her a big favor by marrying her. No comparison to his first wife, that's for sure," the first woman said.

Annie shrunk in her chair, humiliated and angry. How dare these women talk about her in such a derisive manner? They didn't know her, but she had to admit they certainly knew Alice. They were probably qualified to make the comparison, but it hurt nonetheless. She landed from the high she was on with a splat. Doubts began to creep their way back into her self-esteem.

Plastering a smile on her face, she stood when she spotted Burke coming back to the table. She faked another smile to Noreen on their way out. Thankfully, she was too busy to really notice.

Annie saw the concern in Burke's eyes, but she just couldn't bring herself to tell him what she'd heard. As soon as they were settled in the truck, she just pretended to sleep.

* * * *

Burke had felt her withdrawal at the restaurant and wondered about it. For once, he knew that it hadn't been anything he'd done. Shrugging his shoulders he drove. Women were complicated creatures, and he certainly didn't have the key to understanding them. His concern turned to happiness though, as he remembered their time in the barn. God, she was an exciting, sexy woman. He was going to have a hard time not wanting her every moment of every day. Thank God, he had a lot of ranch work to keep him busy night and day.

His smile grew as he pictured her introducing herself to his roan. He'd make time for her no matter what. She needed to know how to ride a horse at least. Hell, there were many things she needed to learn about the ranch. She seemed more than willing to learn and that made Burke proud. For the first time in a long time, he felt very optimistic about his future and of the future his ranch.

He would form a friendship with Annie. They'd be partners in all things except for love. Lots of people did it. He just needed to figure out the right balance between sex and partnership. He knew she expected affection, but he couldn't risk it. He knew he would end up feeling more for her than he wanted. She should be pregnant soon and then all her time would be taken up raising the child. Sounded perfectly logical, but he wondered why he didn't feel happy about it.

Arriving at the ranch house, Burke opened Annie's door and lifted her out. She had blue circles under her eyes, which made her look so tired.

He carried into the house and up the stairs. She didn't weigh very much. Gently, he laid her on the bed and began undressing her, kissing each section of skin he uncovered. Before long, he uncovered everything, and she cried out in need. Burke obliged her, slowly and tenderly. He held her close, sensing her desire for that closeness.

Holding her after sex was different than a loving hug. He was already separating the two, sex and partnership. Things would be fine.

* * * *

Annie felt relaxed and protected in Burke's arms. She lazily dragged her fingers through his chest hair. She knew that he must have been wondering about the scars on her back since he had just kissed every one of them. She felt that she needed to be honest with him, and he made her feel as if she could tell him anything.

"I guess you've noticed the scars on my back," she said quietly. She could feel Burke stiffen beside her. "My stepfather thought that little girls should be seen and not heard. Unfortunately I was more of a tomboy than a ballerina and he punished me for it." Burke's big strong hands ran up and down her back reassuring her. "He used to beat me… a lot. My mother left all discipline matters to him. She constantly told me that I deserved it for being such an evil brat. I was constantly nervous because I didn't seem to know the rules no matter what they were. He changed them daily. If I answered him, I was talking back. If I didn't answer him, I was showing disrespect."

"I've come to believe that he just wanted me naked cowering in front of him. He seemed to relish the power he held over me. He enjoyed hitting me with his belt. In fact he made me remove the belt each and every time." She looked up at Burke and the sympathy she saw reflected in his eyes was her undoing. Tears ran down her face.

"I wasn't bad, Burke, I wasn't."

Burke pulled her tightly against him. "Of course you weren't, honey. You are goodness, light, and certainly not evil. My God, you were just a tiny girl. You did nothing wrong, darlin'. He was the evil one, he, your mother, even your stepbrother. You are safe with me Annie, always."

Annie felt the beginning of healing in her little girl's heart. No one had ever told her it wasn't her fault. She had a lot of thinking to do, but she felt exhausted at the moment. Her last thought before she drifted off to sleep was how Burke had called her goodness and light.

Chapter Six

Annie busily made the morning coffee. It had taken some doing, but she had finally gotten up before Burke and she liked it. There was a certain intimacy waking up in bed with your husband. He'd given her a big kiss, against protests from Cat, and she was amazed that he was hard as a rock in the morning. Annie had wanted to stay in bed, but Burke made promises for the night to come and got dressed. Her face felt warm as she thought of how Adonis-like he looked, getting out of bed naked. Feeling her face grow increasingly hotter, she realized that she lusted after her husband. She smiled wickedly.

The phone rang, jolting her out of her naughty thoughts.

"Annie? It's Sherry I was just about to go berry picking and I wondered if you wanted to come along?"

Annie was thrilled. "I'd like that a lot. I have to confess that I've never picked berries before."

Sherry laughed. "Somehow I didn't think so. After we pick the berries we can make jam."

"Seriously?"

"What you don't like jam?" Sherry asked.

"No. I mean yes I like jam. It's just that I've always wanted to make jam. What time should I be there?"

"Anytime, but the earlier the better since it's too hot in the afternoon to be out in the Texas sun picking berries."

"I'll be there soon. Sherry? Thanks for inviting me."

"It'll be fun. See you in a bit."

She'd wanted to get to know Sherry better, and the jam making was definitely the cherry on top. She couldn't wait to tell Burke her plans.

She poured his coffee when he walked into the kitchen, and he gave her a quick kiss. She'd been waiting all her life for affection. She'd hoped for more. Reaching out she hugged him.

Burke disentangled himself from her. "The day's a-wastin', darlin'." He sat down and ate the eggs she made. "You're spoiling me, you know. You're a good cook."

Annie sat down to join him. "Sherry called. She asked me to go berry picking with her and then she's going to show me how to make jam."

"If I had known just how happy jam makes you, I'd have bought a truckload," he joked. "I'll drive you over."

"That's okay; I'll just drive myself over."

"I said I'll drive you." Burke stared her down.

Annie eyes narrowed as she looked at Burke. "Which is it?" she demanded. "Do you need the truck or am I not allowed to go out on my own?"

Burke wiped his mouth with his napkin and threw it down on his plate. He ran his fingers through his brown hair. "I need the truck today."

Annie simply nodded and turned away, cleaning the kitchen. Somehow, she didn't believe him completely. She still had a sinking suspicion that he just didn't trust her and it made her wonder if it had anything to do with Alice. She was tired of paying for Alice's mistakes. Maybe Sherry would tell her more about the whole situation.

* * * *

Annie was delighted with Sherry's house. The decor was an updated country style. Everything looked so cheerful, colorful with splashes of blue, and yellow. She planned to make a few changes in her house. She could even make new curtains and maybe a sofa cover or two. Sherry greeted her like an old friend and it filled Annie with warmth.

"I love your decor," Annie commented as she walked through the house.

"I like to go antiquing on the weekends. I hit a few flea markets too," she explained. "You're welcome to come anytime you want. I know that Ted just humors me by going and it would be fun to go with a girl friend."

Annie smiled at Sherry. "Thanks I'd like that."

They spent the morning picking berries. Annie had never seen so many berries in one place and she certainly had never picked them before. She and Sherry both laughed at her enthusiasm.

Sherry assured her that in a few years Annie would look upon it as a chore, but Annie didn't agree.

Making jam had always been a dream of hers. Unfortunately, her family discouraged such things. Their cook had, however, taught her to cook thankfully.

She stirred the bubbling mixture of berries, sugar, and pectin. "This is fun, Sherry. Thank you so much for inviting me!"

Sherry smiled. "I'm glad you're having fun. This is just one batch of many," she explained. "We also have a lot of fruit trees on our land. I can make jams with that fruit too." When Annie's look turned hopeful, she just laughed. "Don't worry; you'll be invited to help with that too."

"Good, I'll look forward to it." Annie began to ladle the jam into the jars. "Did Alice help you make jam?" she asked.

Sherry became noticeably silent. "No, she wasn't interested."

"You didn't like her," Annie observed.

Sherry hesitated again. "We were never friends, since she wasn't into country people." She sighed and paused a moment. "To tell you the truth, she was a snob of the first order and I always felt as though she looked down on me and Ted. I tried, for Burke's sake, to be friendly, but she made it hard. After a while we just didn't spend much time with her or Burke for that matter." Sherry took Annie's hand, "That's why we were thrilled to meet you. You're exactly the kind of wife Burke needs."

Annie enjoyed the compliment. She hoped that she was what Burke needed, but she just wasn't sure. There were times that she felt positive that she was good for Burke, but then her doubts crept in. "Do you happen to know if Alice ever cheated on Burke?"

Sherry locked her gaze on Annie. "I don't have proof and I don't like to carry tales, but something happened. I do know that she stayed out at all times of night and Burke went crazy at first looking for her. What she did or where she went, I never asked. I didn't want to know,"

Annie got up and stared out the kitchen window. "That explains a lot." She sighed and turned towards Sherry. The concern that Annie saw in her eyes touched her heart.

Suddenly they both turned to the stove at once. The smell of burning jam had caught their attention. Sherry rushed over and took the pot off the stove.

Annie groaned. "I can't seem to do anything right. Maybe I'm not the type of wife Burke needs after all."

Sherry hugged her. "You are the best thing that has happened to that hard headed man. Don't you forget it." She stepped back and laughed. "Speaking of hard headed men, yours is coming up the walk."

He stepped into the kitchen and Annie walked right up to him and gave him a long kiss. She could tell that he was surprised, but she wasn't going to let that witch of an ex-wife come between them.

"I picked berries and made jam." She felt proud of her accomplishments.

Burke kept her in his arms and looked around the kitchen. "Sure looks like you've been busy." His nose twitched at the smell of burnt jam.

"It was the best time, Burke. Just as I imagined it would be. I can't wait until the fruit trees are ready," she said excitedly.

Sherry smiled, watching them both. "I'll bring by your share when it sets up," she said.

Annie was pleasantly surprised. "I didn't realize…"

Sherry chuckled. "We do fruit here and vegetables at your place."

Annie withdrew from Burke's arms and felt her face pale. "I don't know how to tell you this, Sherry, but we might not have many vegetables this year."

Sherry gave her a puzzled look.

Annie's face grew red now. "I weeded the garden and I mistakenly, not on purpose, mind you…" she rambled.

Burke chuckled. "What she's trying to say is that instead of picking weeds, she picked most of the vegetable plants."

Sherry took Annie's hand in hers, and gave it a quick squeeze. "I'll be over next week and we can fix your garden. It's still early enough in the season to start over," she reassured her.

"Thank you Sherry, I'd appreciate it." Annie gave Burke a sidelong glance. "Someone acted so upset by my mistake that I didn't know that it could be fixed."

Sherry waved a colorful towel at the couple. "You two shoo now. I have housework to do. Day's 'a-wastin'."

Annie gave her a quick hug and followed Burke she out the door. "Does everyone say day's 'a-wastin' around here?" she asked.

"Just about," Burke replied with an amused grin as he opened up her car door for her.

* * * *

The next few days went by peacefully for both Burke and Annie. Annie tried to be patient with Burke's possessiveness. She didn't ask to use the car, but she often took long walks around the ranch and was purposely not immediately accessible to Burke at all times. He didn't like it, but he seemed to accept her need to be alone at times. He never said a word to her about not being able to find her at home.

Annie walked along a wooded path behind the house. She loved the smell of the outdoors, the pungent smell of the pine trees, the soft fragrance of the flowers, and the fresh scent of grass. She breathed deeply, enjoying her walk. She held a bouquet of wildflowers, blue bonnets and Indian paintbrushes, that she'd found on her journey.

As she got closer to the house, she spied Burke in the barn. He looked glorious without his shirt. Her pulse quickened. Their nights together had been spectacular. She smiled, realizing that if she hurried she might be able to seduce her husband before he got too involved in some project.

Annie tipped toed into the barn, eyeing Burke's strong shoulders and back. He was so male, so very virile. Her nipples tightened and her breasts felt heavy in response to his blatant masculinity. She wanted him and it felt wickedly wanton as she snuck up behind him and grabbed his rear end.

He turned in surprise and grabbed her up into his arms. Playfully he peppered her face with kisses as she squealed to be put down.

Burke yelped as he lost his balance and they both landed on the hard ground. Fortunately, Burke was on the bottom. He steeled his arms around Annie and drew her into a long passionate kiss. Suddenly, he rolled them both so that he lay on top. Neither of them seemed to mind the dirt floor as they continued to explore each other's mouths. They were slow to release each other as they heard a truck horn honking in the yard. "Damn," Burke muttered. He let Annie go and stood up.

"What is it?" she asked, pushing her riot of auburn hair away from her face.

Before she could even get up from the floor, one of Burke's cowboys, Nash Crosby, rushed into the barn. He looked apologetically at Burke. It was obvious that he realized what he just broken up.

"We've got four cows bogged down in the east pasture, Boss, and Dan, Surly and Yates are all checking fences to the west," he explained.

"I could sure use your help getting them out," he said hurriedly. He breathed hard as though he had run all the way to the barn instead of driving to it.

Annie realized that it must be important ranch business from Nash's look of alarm. She tried to look understanding as Burke sent her a look of regret. They'd have tonight and the next night and the next. Annie mentally berated herself, watching Burke drive away. She was turning into such a hussy. She smiled nonetheless. As long as they were both happy…

When she walked out of the barn, she noticed a car coming up the long drive. It looked like whoever was driving was in a hurry and she hoped that it wasn't more ranch business.

Annie waited at the barn door as the sleek black convertible came to a screeching halt before her. A woman got out of the car and her beauty stunned Annie. She watched, mesmerized, as the woman pulled off her red silk scarf revealing perfectly styled blonde hair. She removed her designer sunglasses with enviable manicured hands, and her eyes underneath were a deep steel gray. Annie couldn't remember ever seeing nails so long or so red. Before Annie could introduce herself, she was cut off.

"Bring my things in and put them in the master bedroom," she commanded. She gave Annie a derisive look, "You're young and dirty, but I must say you're probably an improvement on Mrs. Harvy."

Annie stared after her, still stunned, watching the woman's hips sway back and forth in her expensive suit. Even if she practiced forever, her hips could never move like that. Annie frowned in dismay. She wasn't completely sure, but she could bet that the glamorous, snobby woman was none other than Alice. Annie ground her teeth. Patting her hair, she found straw embedded in it. She didn't know if she should laugh or cry at the first impression she had made on the other woman. Annie looked down at her clothes and to her horror, she saw that they were painted up and down in dirt.

Well, that's what you get for rolling around on the ground. Leaving the bags right where they were, Annie made her way into the house.

She walked in to find Alice making herself a cup of tea. "Help yourself," Annie said sarcastically. The sight of the other woman in her kitchen put her on edge.

Alice's eyebrows raised, she obviously wasn't used to such a tone. "I beg your pardon?" she asked, pinning Annie in place with her intense stare. "I am home, honey. I live here. I'm sure my husband will let you know who the boss around here is, and it isn't him." She looked past Annie and indignantly put her hands on her hips. "Where are my bags?" she demanded. She took a step closer to Annie attempting to intimidate her.

Annie's eyes narrowed as she glared at Alice. "I don't know who you think you are. I live here, not you."

Alice waved her hand in the air, dismissing what Annie said. "Sure, whatever. Burke never did have good luck with housekeepers." She turned toward the stairs. "Just do as you're told and bring in my things."

Annie sputtered as she watched Alice walk upstairs. Alice could go to hell and so could her bags. She wanted Burke, she needed Burke, but who knew when he'd be home? She had no idea how long it took to get cattle unbogged or whatever they were. Huffing in aggravation, she grabbed Cat and walked out of the house. She didn't want to have another confrontation with that woman. Besides, she would have noticed by now that Burke obviously lived with another woman. All of Annie's things were in the master bedroom.

Annie heard Alice yell. She probably made it to the bedroom. Well, too damn bad for Alice, She had horses she needed to introduce herself to. There was no way she was going back into that house without Burke. But, Annie did feel a pang of envy. The women at the diner were right; there was no comparison between her and Alice. Alice was a beauty and she was nothing but plain. She wondered if it bothered Burke that she wasn't beautiful. Did he find her lacking? She certainly wasn't a big-boobed Barbie like Alice, but what did he think?

Annie wasn't in the mood to talk to the horses. She wasn't even in the mood to watch Cat play. Even though Alice was an impossible wench, Annie couldn't shake the fact that Burke had once loved her.

She couldn't bring herself to go back into the house. She felt so helpless and disgusted. That was her house, Burke was her husband, and she knew that she needed to go in there and have it out with that adulterer of a woman. She should have set Alice straight as soon as she treated her as a servant. Just who did she think she was calling Burke her husband?

Annie dug deep and found her strength. She was not going to let Alice ruin her life. *No way in hell*, she chanted to herself. She picked up Cat and made her way back to the house. The motto: *never let them see you sweat*, popped into her mind. Her mouth turned up into a slight smile. Taking a deep breath, she felt as though she was going into her first cage match. She hated confrontations and she'd had enough violence in her life, but she had to face Alice or she would never be able to look at herself in the mirror again.

Annie entered the house and found Alice sitting at the kitchen table flipping through a fashion magazine. She'd taken off her designer suit jacket and Annie could see her breasts practically falling out of her push up bra. Her silk blouse was unbuttoned practically to her belly button and it was disgusting. But Annie did have to admit that the red blouse perfectly matched Alice's nail polish, which perfectly matched her lipstick. She felt at a disadvantage in her dirty T-shirt and jeans. She knew that her hair looked a colossal mess, but now wasn't the time to cry about spilled milk. She set Cat on the floor and watched her take off as if the devil chased her.

Annie straightened her shoulders and looked Alice right in the eye. "I think there's been some mistake here," she began, trying to sound calm and cool.

Alice laughed at her. "Don't worry, honey; I threw all of your things out of my bedroom." She looked back down at her magazine as if Annie didn't matter. Before Annie made a reply, Alice suggested that she might want to get her dirty clothes out of the hallway before Burke got home.

A pit formed in Annie's stomach and she wanted to run. Alice's sharp tongue could make even Sonny cry. She didn't have the arsenal to fight this woman, but she didn't have a choice. "Burke is *my* husband," she said in warning.

Alice looked her up and down and laughed. "Nice try, sweetheart, but you're too ugly and definitely not womanly enough for Burke. He likes big busted, curvy women who won't scare him when he looks at them over the breakfast table," she said scathingly. "He might be taking you to his bed, but I bet it's always with the lights off."

Annie gasped.

"Alice, that's enough!" Burke commanded as he walked into the room. He gave her a scornful look and went to Annie, pulling her close to his side. She knew he could feel her trembling. "Annie is my wife and you should have a care what you say to her," he warned.

Alice completely changed when she caught sight of Burke. She squealed in delight and rushed over to him, practically knocking over her chair in her hurry. "Darling, it's so good to see you again," she gushed. She took Burke's hand and adeptly separated the married couple. "I drove all day just to catch a look of you, Burke." Laughing, she wrapped her arms around his neck. She sighed, loudly kissing him with relish.

Annie watched in horror while Alice kissed her husband. Her little sighs were like tiny daggers to Annie's heart. She knew that Burke was strong enough to set Alice away from him, but he didn't, and it made her want to rip every bleached blonde hair off Alice's head. Her fury turned to sickness as she realized that Burke wasn't fighting the kiss at all.

She couldn't contain the sob of distress she made. She flew out the kitchen door. She wasn't going to hide in the barn again, so she just sat on the porch steps, looking out at the land she'd grown to love. The days were growing longer and the sun had yet to set.

Annie gazed at her favorite roses. She loved to see them dance as the cooling breeze went through them. Maybe her marriage was a mistake after all. She closed her eyes, replaying the kiss between Burke and Alice. She sat on the step not knowing if she waited for Burke to tell her either their marriage was over or the kiss was all a big mistake. Either scenario could happen. After all, Burke never claimed to love her. She laid her head on her knees and waited.

* * * *

Burke's disentangled himself from Alice, and wiped his mouth in disgust. "What the hell are you doing here?" he demanded.

Alice simply smiled at him. He hated her smiles; they usually worked in the past.

"I came here for a reconciliation. I realize now how wrong I was to walk away from you." Walking toward him again, she placed her hand on his chest. He flinched, but that didn't seem to deter her.

"We were so good together, remember?" she asked huskily. "I've missed you dreadfully." She batted her eyelashes and she gave him a pleading look. "I need you, Burke. I need you like I've never needed anyone before."

"I'm married, happily married," he responded. "You're going to have to leave."

Tears welled up in her steel gray eyes. "I can respect that Burke. I just need a place to stay for a few weeks." She let her tears fall freely. "Please, Burke," she pleaded. "I have nowhere else to go. I used the last of my cash to put gas in my car to get here."

Burke ran his fingers through his hair. He didn't want her here, but he couldn't turn her out either. He knew that the next few weeks would be a living hell, but as her ex-husband, he felt a certain responsibility toward her. He shouldn't, but he did.

"All right," he agreed, sighing deeply. "You can stay, but just for two weeks, and I want you to help Annie around the house. This isn't a bed and breakfast. Understand?"

Alice's tears quickly evaporated and she laughed in delight. She threw herself at Burke covering his face with kisses. "I'll be good," she promised, "you won't even know I'm here."

Burke highly doubted that, but he didn't know what else to do. Right now, his main concern was Annie; he'd seen how hurt she was before she went outside. How he was going to manage the next two weeks he didn't know, but he had to reassure Annie.

He saw her sitting on the steps and braced himself. He didn't know what to say. From the look of things, they weren't getting along when he came home. He wasn't sure if Annie could defend herself from Alice's sharp claws. He knew from experience just how mean and spiteful she could be. Why in God's name did he tell her she could stay? Shaking his head, he started for the door and felt Alice right behind him.

He turned toward her. "Annie and I need to talk alone."

She gave him her pouty look, but right now, he didn't care. He needed to make things right with his wife.

* * * *

Annie heard the screen door slam. She felt so weary. All she wanted in this world was peace and love. Right now, she had neither and she felt crushed. Things were going so well between them and now... Annie was afraid, afraid that she was going to lose Burke. Alice was so beautiful. Well, at least until she opened her mouth and then any beauty disappeared. Burke sat beside her and put his arm around her.

"I'm sorry, darlin'," he said, his voice full of regret.

Annie shrugged his arm off her shoulder and stood up whipping her head around to face him. "Don't you dare call me that again! She calls you that!"

Burke frowned. "She calls me darling. I call you darlin'."

"Same thing!"

"Believe me Annie there is a world of difference, but that isn't why I came out to talk to you." He stood up at the bottom of the stairs and grabbed her hand. "Let's go somewhere where we can talk alone."

Apprehensively, Annie let him help her up and began to walk hand in hand with him. She knew that she was trembling and it shamed her. She walked with him, breathing in the scent of him. He smelled of leather, spice, and masculine sensuality. He also smelled of hard work and the outdoors. Closing her eyes, she willed herself to make a memory of his scent for when they were no longer together. It wasn't fair, she lamented to herself. Alice had no right to come back. Burke was her husband now.

She realized that Burke had stopped walking. Annie looked up into his sky blue eyes and saw unhappiness and deep regret. Mentally bracing herself for what was to come; she straightened her spine and raised her chin, waiting for the blow.

To her surprise, he stoked her cheek. .His gentleness was the last straw. Embarrassed, Annie turned away to try and hide the tears welling up in her eyes. She fought fiercely to get herself together. It had been an awful day with that woman showing up. She knew deep down that she wasn't the type of wife Burke needed. He needed someone made of sterner stuff, not some wilting ninny like her.

Annie wanted to tell him that she loved him, but she refused to make a fool out of herself. She shuddered as she felt Burke's warm hands on her shoulders. It felt as though he was lending his support to her and she wished it were so.

"Shhhh, Annie," he murmured. He wrapped his arms around her waist and pulled her back snug against his strong chest. He kissed the side of her neck, causing her to shiver.

"She can be a spiteful bitch, and I'm sorry that she unleashed her anger on you," he said, holding her tight.

Annie felt so protected in his brawny arms. The feel of his strong hard chest made her stomach feel as though it was full of butterflies.

"I'm just so edgy today."

She turned in his arms and laid her head against his chest. She finally calmed her breathing and drew back enough to look at him, blushing at his smile. It was unexpected. She laid her head against him again and sighed as he rubbed her back up and down. He was the only one in her whole life who had ever held her when she cried and she wanted to prolong the soothing feeling.

"Annie," he said hesitantly. "Alice will be staying with us for two weeks."

Annie pushed against his broad chest to put distance between them. Sparks practically flew from her hurt eyes. "No way in hell!"

Burke looked quickly at the house hoping that they weren't overheard. "Please, keep your voice down. I don't want Alice to know our business. Annie, I know that we're just beginning to make our way as a married couple, but Alice has no place to go."

"Like that's our problem?" she demanded, folding her arms in front of her.

"Unfortunately, as much as I hate the idea of her being here, I feel a sense of obligation toward her." Burke ran his fingers through his brown hair. He cupped her cheek in his large work worn hand, cradling it, beseeching her with his eyes to understand.

"I know it doesn't make sense, but it's just the kind of man I am, the kind that I've always strived to be, a man with compassion and integrity, a man who doesn't turn his back on his obligations no matter how distasteful they may be. Unfortunately I see Alice as an obligation that I can't turn away."

She rubbed her cheek against his hand. Reaching up for his hand, she kissed it lovingly. "Only two weeks, right?" she asked quietly.

"Only two weeks," Burke agreed as he drew her back into his arms and kissed her. He backed her up against the corral fence. Kissing her deeply, he started to unsnap her jeans but stopped when they heard the unmistakable sound of the screen door slam.

"We'll get through this, honey," he whispered.

Annie jabbed him in the ribs with her elbow. "We'd better, cowboy," she replied. "I guess I have a mess outside our bedroom to clean up. I don't suppose her highness would have put everything back?"

Burke grinned at her. "I wouldn't bank on it." He grabbed her hand and walked her inside.

****

The next morning Annie rose with a smile on her face. Burke had been right. It took more than an hour to put her belongings back into the master bedroom especially with Cat helping, but they were back where they belonged. Burke cleaned the kitchen and Annie had no idea what Alice did. She didn't care. She'd been the recipient of some good ol' cowboy lovin' last night. At least that's what Burke had called it. As far as she was concerned, her cowboy could give her some lovin' anytime. Not even Alice's sour face could bring her down. She felt too satisfied.

True to form, Alice didn't know how to cook and wanted Annie to wait on her. Annie made her eggs, toast, and served it up with a smile. Somehow, it seemed to infuriate Alice, but Annie didn't care.

Walking toward the back door Annie heard Alice call to her. Fixing another smile on her face, she turned around. "What?"

"I heard that a mama cat gave birth last night in the hay loft. I just thought that you'd want to see them."

Annie studied the other woman. Shrugging her shoulders, she turned and left. It seemed almost too tempting to run to the barn and see the kittens, but she could see Alice watching her from the window. Walking over to her pitiful garden, Annie pretended to be looking it over, bending over and picking what she hoped was a weed.

That woman was dictating her every move, even when she wasn't ordering her around. Annie decided that if she wanted to see the kittens then she'd do just that, no matter who watched. How Burke ever put up with that barracuda she would never know.

It was quiet at the ranch this morning. The only sound was the rusty old metal windmill turning. It creaked something awful. She hadn't really noticed before. She would have to ask Burke what it was used for.

Smiling she went into the barn. She'd become quite comfortable with all the animals. She loved greeting each horse and she didn't care who laughed. The horses seemed to enjoy her attention.

She made her way over to the ladder that led to the hayloft. She was a bit suspicious. After all, why would Alice be so nice? And for that matter, she seemed to hate cats.

Annie examined each rung of the ladder before she climbed up it, shaking her head at how paranoid she'd become. It was going to be hard, but she'd just have to ride hurricane Alice out. It was the only thing she could do short of leaving the ranch.

Confident that the ladder was completely safe, she climbed up into the hayloft. Hay was everywhere, bales, and bales along with loose hay on the floor. A small aisle appeared between the piled bales. Annie started down the aisle and felt something snap painfully around her ankle.

Crying out, she reached down and felt metal, agonizingly clamped around her foot. She could see blood from her broken skin and she felt like swooning. Tears filled her eyes and she was afraid to move.

The more she looked, the more she realized that it was some sort of animal trap. Reaching down she tried to pry the trap open only to have it open slightly and reclose on her ankle. Her heart raced and she began to panic. Were there more traps up here? Damn that Alice! She'd been after Burke from the very first.

She honestly didn't know what to do. She yelled until her throat was raw, but no one answered. Burke said he'd be back for lunch and she hoped to God that he kept his word. Anything could happen to delay him. Suddenly she heard a noise from below. "Help!"

"Annie is that you?" Alice called.

Annie gritted her teeth and put a lid on her temper, she needed help, and it didn't matter who gave it to her. "I'm up here I'm stuck!"

Alice's blonde head finally became visible as she climbed up the ladder. "What in the world?"

"Just help me get this thing off."

"Well, how am I supposed to do that? What the hell is that thing?"

Annie's patience ended. "It's an animal trap. I need you to help me pry it open!"

If she hadn't been the one in pain, she would have laughed at the way Alice looked at the trap and then at her long nails.

"Just get over here and help me!"

"You don't have to yell you know."

"Listen if you don't get over here and help me I'm going to pull out every hair on your head!"

"What in God's name is going on up there?" Burke shouted as he quickly climbed the ladder. He took one look and pushed Alice out of the way. "Oh my God. How did this happen? What are you doing up here?"

"Just get it off!" Annie yelled.

"Hold still, love." He got down on his knees and used all his strength to pry it open. Gently, he took Annie's ankle in his hand and examined it.

He helped her to a sitting position and he wrapped her ankle in his red bandana. He kissed her cheek and spoke soothingly to her. "At least it's not broken."

Turning to Alice, he frowned. "Alice, you're here in heels? Really?"

Her mouth started to look pouty. "I heard screaming and I came as fast as I could. I'm here to help. Don't yell at me!"

"Well, could you please go down the ladder and get Nash? He should be up in my office," he asked.

"Well, of course. I'm here to help," she reiterated as she gingerly made her way down the ladder in her spiked shoes.

"I can't believe you use traps like these!" Annie accused tearfully.

"Oh, sweetheart, I don't. Heck I don't even know where this one came from."

"I hear you need some help," Nash said, coming up and looking from Burke to Annie. "What happened?"

"Have you seen this trap before?" Burke asked him.

Nash took off his hat and scratched his head. "Seems to me that's the one that was hanging on the wall in the tack room. It's always been there. I figured it was a tribute to older times."

"You're right we do have all the old tools and stuff hanging on the wall. Help me get Annie down the ladder."

It wasn't easy, but they managed to do it. Burke swept her up into his arms and took her to the house. He bypassed Alice and went straight into his office, nodding Nash in and Alice out.

He gently placed Annie on the couch. "Nash, get the first aid kit and some ice, will you?"

"Sure thing, boss."

"Don't let Alice in here when you come back."

"You can count on me."

"Annie, what happened?"

"I don't know. Alice told me about kittens in the hayloft and you know me. I'm a sucker for a kitten. I was a bit wary since it was Alice's idea. I checked the ladder."

"The ladder?"

"I figured she rigged it so that I'd fall or something, but it wasn't until I started down the aisle that I stepped on that trap."

Burke looked pensive as he sat on the couch with her feet in his lap. "I know you want to blame Alice, but I don't think she did it."

Annie was astonished. "Why not?" she demanded, feeling hurt that he didn't believe her.

"She simply isn't strong enough to set the trap. It's that simple," he explained.

"Well, if she didn't do it then who did? What about the kittens she told me about? There aren't any kittens in that loft. She knew she was sending me into danger," she insisted.

Examining his face, Annie realized that Burke didn't agree with her. She could tell that he didn't think it was Alice. It didn't surprise her, but it hurt.

"It's a good thing that the foot trap didn't have teeth. It would have torn your foot to shreds."

Shivering at the thought, Annie agreed. Her ankle was cut and bruised, but she didn't think it was sprained. It just hurt.

A day with ice on it should do it, she mused. It still galled her to no end that he didn't believe her about Alice's involvement. It could be that she wasn't strong enough, but Alice sent her up there. However it happened, she had to be a part of it.

Nash came in and handed Burke the first aid kit. He put a bowl of warm water on the table and a bag of ice next to it. "Well, if that's all you need, I want to check around in the barn. If there was one trap there may be more. It could have happened to anyone who was up in the hayloft. It doesn't sit right with me."

"Me neither. Thanks for taking care of it, Nash. Let me know if you find anything," Burke said.

Nash tipped his hat to Annie and left. "He's a nice man," she commented.

Burke grinned at her. "Do I have reason to be jealous?"

"Just fix my ankle. Day's 'a-wastin' you know."

Burke laughed a deep rolling laugh. Then he grew serious. "This is going to hurt," he said, putting the antiseptic on her ankle.

Annie stiffened and she cried out. After a minute, she finally relaxed, and Burke propped her leg up on a pillow, covering her ankle with ice.

"It's not that I don't believe you, Annie. Someone hurt you and I'm going to get to the bottom of it. In fact, I'm going to talk to

Alice now." Leaning down he kissed her on the lips, lingering a bit before he stood back up. "I'll be by later to check on you."

"Thank you."

"Day's a-wastin'." He smiled at her.

Her smile left as she watched him leave the room. Why didn't he take her word? He acted as though she was a crazy old cat lady. Alice did this, she just knew it and her phony help wasn't going to fool Annie.

Burke would find out she was right. Annie felt confident that he would.

* * * *

Burke didn't know what to think. Alice claimed that she hadn't said a word about kittens to Annie. She kept insisting that she hated cats. Burke knew that was true, but if she hadn't done it, then who?

His frustration was deep. Alice looked sincere, yet Annie insisted that Alice sent her into the barn. He and Nash had examined the trap and they both agreed that Alice wouldn't have been able to set it herself. It left them both with a very uneasy feeling. Someone had set it, maybe not to hurt Annie, but they had planned to hurt someone.

"It worries me, Nash. I don't know one man on the ranch that would have done such a thing."

"I know, Boss, it'd be easiest to blame Alice, but dang it, she couldn't have done it, not with her long nails and high heels. All we can do is keep our eyes open. I'll talk to the men when they come in later."

"Thanks, Nash. I appreciate your help." Burke said, running his fingers through his hair. "I have to go and try to convince my wife that Alice didn't try to kill her. I have a feeling that she's not going to take it well."

"I don't envy you there, that's for sure."

"Talk to you later." Burke walked back to the house. He dreaded having to tell Annie that Alice couldn't have done it, and he still wasn't sure about the whole kitten story. Nothing made sense.

Alice met him at the door with a bright smile on her face. "Did you find out who put that nasty trap in the hayloft?"

Burke shook his head.

"You don't believe it was me? Annie must have heard something wrong. I never mentioned kittens to her. In fact, I really don't remember talking to her much this morning. You know she wishes me gone. Maybe she did it herself."

Burke gave her a long stare. "No, she didn't do it. You didn't do it. Neither of you are strong enough to set that trap. Maybe you did tell her that they were kittens. I don't know what to think. Just stay out of my wife's way."

"Sure, Burke. Whatever you say, darling."

Burke wanted to roll his eyes at her, but he just nodded and walked down the hall to his office. His heart turned over as he saw Annie asleep on the couch. The ice bag and pillow were on the floor and her beautiful auburn hair looked so sexy all tousled around her. He liked her disheveled look. It made him wonder if her ankle would interfere with making love. His body swelled with desire. Slowly he bent down and kissed her, nibbling at her bottom lip.

A small sigh of pleasure escaped from her as her eyes opened. Burke smiled into her green eyes and took her into his arms. Her lips were so soft, so pliant, so amazing. The kiss was breathtaking.

He felt her trying to talk under his lips and he pulled away. "What?" he groaned.

"Let me sit up," she said.

Burke pulled away and helped her to sit up on the couch. He sat down next to her when she made room for him. He moved closer to her intending to kiss her again.

"Wait! What about the trap? Did you send Alice packing?"

"Well, not exactly," he began.

Annie looked at him as if he had two heads. "I'm afraid to ask, but what in the name of heaven does that mean?"

Burke winced at her outrage. Whatever happened to his concept of a nice easy uncomplicated marriage for the production of children? "There is no physical way Alice could have set that trap. It takes a lot of strength to open it. I know she isn't strong from doing any work."

"*Harrumph.* So she walks away clean. It was my imagination that she told me about the kittens. I'm the crazy one. I guess I imagined the painful trap too. Well, at least I know where I stand. As far as pecking order or anything else, I am at the very bottom! No, don't even say anything, Burke. I can tell by the look in your eyes that you don't believe me. Somehow, I thought my life with you was going to be different, but it's not. No one ever believed me before, thanks to Sonny. Now, I don't even know what to say. I suppose I shouldn't say anything."

Burke's heart turned over. "Annie, please don't take on so."

"Take on so? Take on so? What is that even supposed to mean?" Sighing, she put her hand up to stop him from answering. "I just want to go and lay down in my bed."

Burke stood up and bent to grab her up into his arms, intent on taking her to their room, but it seemed that Annie had other ideas. She pushed him away as though his touch repulsed her. Burke watched her limp out of the room, his heart heavy. He'd handled it all wrong. Sitting back on the couch, he ran his hand over his face. Annie was right; he should never have told her that he doubted her. She was his wife and she was entitled to a certain consideration.

* * * *

Annie stayed in her room for the rest of the day. It didn't surprise her that no one bothered to check on her. She wasn't as important as the ranch. Burke had made that abundantly clear. In fact, she was not as important as Alice either. He must still have had feelings for that witch. It wasn't fair. She had wholeheartedly believed that this was her turn for a bit of happiness.

That night, Burke slid into bed and pulled her close. It was late and she didn't even know what time it was. No one asked if she wanted any dinner. She never thought she could feel so hurt by this man. She had trusted him. She'd given him her heart and lately it seemed as though he wanted to give it back. The pain in her heart became excruciating.

Burke held her as she ignored him, stroking her back and murmuring to her. She just lay there in the circle of his arms wondering how much longer he would be coming to her bed. "I'm sorry," she whispered brokenly.

"You have nothing to be sorry for, honey."

Annie shook her head. "I'm not the wife you want. I've been such a fool. I wanted something so badly that I imagined it to be true."

"What would that be?"

"I thought that you were happy with me. I thought we'd be able to build a life together, to have children."

"Annie, I am sorry about today. I have been so focused on finding out what happened that I didn't even consider your feelings. What I should have done is let you know that you come first, before the ranch and anyone on it. I don't know if I've ever been as happy as I am with you. We are going to build a life together, we will have a family, and we will be happy. I know I hurt your feelings and when you refused to come down for dinner I felt awful."

"I didn't refuse dinner, it was never offered."

"Alice... I'm such a fool."

Annie leaned over and kissed him. "Make love to me, Burke. Make my doubts go away," she pleaded.

"Woman, it would be my pleasure."

Annie could feel her worth in the tender way he made love to her. He almost brought her to tears with his gentleness. Everything was going to be okay she knew it. She could feel it.

* * * *

"Mrs. Harvy doesn't work here anymore?" Alice questioned the next morning after breakfast.

"Not since I've been here," Annie replied.

Alice laughed as though she had shared a private joke with herself. "Oh, darling. This is rich!" she exclaimed, as she got up from the table towering over Annie. "It all makes perfect sense. I just wish I had known about it when I got here, and then maybe my feelings wouldn't have been so hurt."

Annie was perplexed. Alice talked in riddles, and she didn't want to know what it all meant.

"Well?" asked Alice. "Oh," she said as she placed a hand over her heart in mock compassion. "You don't know do you? You poor dear, you see it's obvious that Burke married you as the unpaid housekeeper." She shook her head and *tsked* a couple of times. "How utterly embarrassing for you dear," she patronized.

Annie was about to lose her temper when she heard a truck drive up. Quickly, she went to the front door, hoping to escape Alice. To her relief, Sherry got out of the truck. Annie limped out of the house to greet her new friend. "I'm so glad to see you." She gave Sherry a big hug.

Sherry hugged her back and gave her a big smile. "I did promise to help replant, didn't I?"

"You most certainly did and you couldn't have come at a better time," Annie assured her.

Sherry looked toward the front door and her jaw dropped. "Surely I'm seeing things," she said, in a whisper.

"Afraid not."

"Well, well, if it isn't Ted's wife. Cher, isn't it?" Alice asked, in her superior voice.

"No Al, its Sherry not Cher," Sherry replied sarcastically, obviously hating the sight of the other woman. "It's very surprising to see you here. I thought with all the money you wrung out of Burke you'd be living the high life somewhere… else."

"Burke never did have much money," Alice retorted.

"Certainly not after you got your hands on it," Sherry shot back angrily.

Annie could feel the tension rising. She turned to Sherry "Let's get started on the garden."

Sherry gave Alice another disgusted look and turned away from her. "Sure. Let me show you all the veggies I brought," she said, in false cheerfulness.

As soon as they were out of earshot of the house, Sherry grabbed Annie. "What in the name of God is going on here?" she demanded.

Annie felt extremely grateful to have a friend to confide in. "She drove up two days ago," she explained. "She told Burke that she was broke and needed a place to stay for two weeks."

Sherry's eyes grew wide. "He agreed to let her stay?" she asked incredulously.

Annie nodded. "He said he still felt an obligation to her and hell I don't know. She's supposed to be out of here in two weeks. I hope I can take her that long." She gave Sherry a sidelong look. "She isn't the nicest woman I've ever met."

"Oh, Lord." Sherry laughed. "She's a viper."

"Yeah I found that out first hand. She told me about a litter of kittens in the hayloft and I stepped on a land trap. Needless to say, there were no kittens."

"You've got to be kidding me! Are you okay? Is that why you're limping?"

Annie was appreciative of Sherry's show of outrage on her behalf. "Yes my ankle is cut and bruised, but I'll be fine."

"What is she still doing here? Surely Burke wouldn't want her here after that!"

"It seems that there is no way that Alice could have set the trap. She's not strong enough. I'm just going to do my best to ignore her."

"Well, if things get too bad, then just come over for a cup of coffee," Sherry offered.

Annie gave her friend a hug. With that, they each grabbed a flat of plants and headed out back. Annie briefly went inside to grab her gloves, hat and sun block and was extremely grateful that Alice was nowhere around.

Annie and Sherry worked side by side with Sherry explaining the finer points of gardening all the while. Annie drank in all of Sherry's advice and knowledge. She was determined to have enough vegetables to can. They laughed and joked, avoiding the topic of Alice for about an hour until they heard the screen door slam.

They both looked up to see Alice coming off the porch, sunglasses and drink in her hand. They watched Alice set up a poolside type of reclining chair, and both women stared. Annie felt a bit envious of the blonde beauty's figure. Her skin was already a soft bronze. Obviously, Alice didn't burn.

The sound of an approaching truck and subsequent slam of the door drew all three of the women's attention. Annie had an urge to get up and run to her husband, despite her leg, needing to feel his reassuring arms around her. Watching as he walked toward the trio, she couldn't help but admire how handsome he was. Even sweaty and dusted from head to toe in ranch dirt he was the sexiest man she had ever seen. Her stomach began to quicken as he moved closer to her. She smiled at him.

Alice stood up and called out to him. Burke stopped and Annie could see them talking. Next thing she knew they went into the house.

Annie felt as though she had been kicked in the stomach. She glanced at Sherry, and the pity she saw in her friend's eyes was almost more than she could take. Her eyes misted as she pretended to be preoccupied with planting her carrots.

Loud laughter came from inside the house. Annie waited for it to stop, but it continued until she lost track of the time. She picked up all of their gardening tools. She couldn't even look at Sherry, feeling too humiliated. Burke hadn't even greed either of them. He only had eyes for Alice. Annie felt sick to her stomach. With her hand over her mouth, she rushed inside the house. She felt bad about not saying good-bye to Sherry, but her need to be sick was too great and she needed to lie down.

Annie ran upstairs and dropped onto her bed, burying her face. When she felt like she could finally get up again, she looked in the mirror and her reflection horrified her. Once again, she was streaked with dirt and sweat. Her hair looked like a rat's nest and her clothes were stained by her day's labor. Sitting on the edge of the tub she wondered whether the physical abuse she felt as a child made her feel any worse than she did now. This was supposed to be her house, her husband, her chance at having a family and her soft place to fall. Burke didn't love her as she had hoped he would. Last night he had almost convinced her with his sweet lovemaking, but he was just fooling himself and her. His heart was otherwise engaged to that blonde bimbo.

Looking in the mirror again, she couldn't blame Burke. She'd always known that she was no prize. Hell, her own family hadn't wanted her. Annie felt so tired and so defeated. Usually she could shake things off, but not this. The worst part was that she had nowhere else to go. She thought about taking a shower and changing but decided against it. It didn't matter anyway.

Slowly she made her way downstairs to be sure that Sherry had left and all the tools were put away. She could hear more laughter coming from the family room as she walked through her kitchen. She went out the back and made her way to her garden.

On any other day, she would have taken great delight in her accomplishments in the garden. Sherry had taught her a lot and they had worked hard, side by side. Despite herself, she smiled a little as she thought of her friend's fury at Burke on her behalf. It felt wonderful to have someone in her corner for a change. Sherry was the type of friend that wouldn't lie or try to deceive her. She had thought that she'd put those types of people behind her, but now there was Alice. As hard as she tried, she just couldn't ignore that woman. She didn't even know how to fight back. She didn't even know if it was worth the fight. If Burke didn't want her… The pain in her heart was too deep. She couldn't think about it anymore.

She watched from the garden as one of the paints rolled on his back. She didn't know that horses even did that. Annie could feel Burke's heat as he stepped behind her. She hoped he wouldn't touch her, but he did, putting his hands on her shoulders. Quickly, she shrugged his hands off and took a few steps away from him, refusing to look at him. His words had a way of melting her heart and right now, she didn't want to hear it.

"Annie, I know that Alice can be a trial. I'm sorry if she did something to upset you."

Annie turned in a flash. "You are so mule headed if you really think that it was Alice that made me so upset. I expect her to try to get to me at every turn, but not you, Burke. Never you."

"If I've done something to upset your delicate sensibilities just say so," he growled.

Annie's angry eyes held Burke's furious ones. "Oh, Burke," she sighed painfully. "Is that what you really think of me, a person with delicate sensibilities?" She pulled her eyes away from his and looked at the horizon, knowing that she didn't expect an answer.

"Maybe I am sensitive," she finally agreed. "If seeing my husband greet his ex-wife and ignore his present wife wasn't enough, then hearing you laugh and joke with your ex-wife was. Did you even know that Sherry and I were right there in the garden? You only had eyes for her and Sherry pitied me for it."

"Annie, I'm so, so sorry. Alice needed help with the dryer. It wouldn't turn on."

Annie looked at him finally and could tell that he was sorry, but somehow it wasn't enough. She turned and walked into the house, took a hot shower and went to bed. She cried herself to sleep that night and she hoped that she cried silently enough, she didn't want Alice to know just how much she was hurt.

* * * *

Burke stood outside and waited for the bedroom light to go off. It amazed him how much work she and Sherry had done in one day. It pleased him that Annie was a real partner in his ranch, their ranch. He admired her work ethic

He didn't know what to say to Annie and she sure as hell didn't want his comfort. Didn't she know that he'd take her, scarred back and all, over the viper he'd married before? His best guess was that she didn't know, he hadn't told her that he loved her. He hadn't wanted to before, but he knew he couldn't help it now. His heart twisted as he recalled Annie's pain filled eyes looking at him accusingly. He wasn't sure how to make things right, but he was going to make sure that Alice didn't get in their way again. He had to admit to himself that it was his fault. He shouldn't have let her entice him. Laughing to himself in disgust, he realized that it was Alice's plan all along. She was poison and he knew it.

Burke walked into the dark house. No light welcomed him and he experienced a great sense of loneliness. He jumped, startled to find Alice sitting at the kitchen table in the dark. He tried to walk past her, but she grabbed his arm.

"I'm sorry that your wife got upset, darling," she purred. "How was I supposed to know that her back was all scarred? I mean compared to me she must feel like a circus freak."

Burke's eyes narrowed and he shook her hand off him. He wondered what her game was and how she knew about the scars. "Let it be, Alice," he warned.

"But, Burke it's not my fault you married a dirty housekeeper. If only you had waited you could have had your trophy wife back," she stated, looking innocent.

Burke laughed harshly. "You're no prize, believe me. That woman lying in my bed right now is ten times the woman that you are, so back off," he strongly cautioned.

"You can't mean that," Alice said as she pouted.

"I said let it be. Good night."

Chapter Seven

Annie groaned as she woke up and realized that the bright Texas sun had been up for a good long time. She'd been sleeping in later this past week, trying to avoid Burke and Alice. For some reason Alice decided that she needed to be up early to keep Burke entertained, while Annie served them breakfast. After the second day, Annie slept in, not wanting to be their cook and server. She sighed, stretching her arms overhead, trying to get the kinks out of her back. She hadn't had a peaceful night of sleep in a week.

Every time Burke touched her, she stiffened and pulled away. Today she was determined to try harder. Alice would be leaving in less than a week and Annie couldn't wait. She didn't know what Alice's plans were, but she didn't care, she considered it not her problem. Burke had promised that Alice would be gone in two weeks and she wholly believed him.

Annie cheered up and dressed in her cutoff jeans and pink T-shirt. She couldn't go on this way with Burke. She walked downstairs determined to find him and put things to rights. Looking out the window, she sipped her coffee wondering if Burke was still around or off cowboying. She smiled to herself. She needed some of that cowboy's love and she needed it now.

It put a bad taste in her mouth when she saw Alice at the kitchen table Annie tried to ignore her. But it looked like Alice had other plans. Her smile looked excessively bright this morning and Annie had a sinking feeling.

"There's a note for you," Alice said, handing it over.

Grabbing the paper out of Alice's hand, Annie walked to the window, turning her back on Alice as she read it. She didn't want Alice to have the pleasure if the news was bad. It was from Burke. It said that he'd be out of town overnight on ranch business. It distressed her that he hadn't told her personally, but on the other hand, he hadn't taken Alice with him.

"Well, we're on our own," Annie said with false pleasantry. "Guess you'll have to make you own meals today."

The look on Alice's face made it all worthwhile. Annie hummed as she walked out the door, planning to take a long walk. It felt so good to be one with nature. It was something that she hadn't even known about living in the city. Pausing under a cottonwood tree, she watched squirrels busy at work. They chattered at each other as the birds looked on and chirped. At one point, she saw two dragonflies in flight, playing a mysterious game.

She didn't want to go back to the house. She didn't trust Alice. It was so obvious that she was trying to break up their marriage. Why couldn't Burke see her for what she was, a spoiled, dangerous woman?

The day grew warmer and she could feel moisture in the air. Rain, she thought as she saw the dark clouds starting to roll through. Luckily, she wasn't far from the house. Hearing the rumble of thunder, she ran to the house only to find the door locked.

Shocked, she tried them again running from the back to the front of the house as the rain pelted down in sheets. They never locked the doors to the house. "Damn you Alice open up!"

Annie saw a shadow at the front window and she just knew it had to be Alice. She pounded on the door, but Alice still wouldn't open the door.

The air started growing colder and the rain continued to pour out of the sky. Thunder vibrated the ground as lightening ignited the sky. Even though she stood on the covered porch, she got soaked.

Deciding that she would be safer in the barn, she ran out into the punishing rain. The wind had really kicked up and once she got into the barn, she had a hard time closing the door.

Leaning against the closed door, Annie was breathless. Water dripped from her soaking body and she shivered. She hated that woman! What right did she have to lock the doors? What a spiteful witch!

Finally catching her breath, Annie walked further into the barn and located a blanket. Without hesitation, she shucked her clothes and wrapped herself in the scratchy blanket.

The walls of the barn were creaking as the wind continued to blow and the rain poured. Burke had told her that the storms out here could be deadly, but she really had to see it to believe it. The animals were getting restless. They seemed to be as anxious as she was.

She walked to the back of the barn to the tack room. Gratefully, she found some clothes there. They were excessively big, but she didn't care. Rolling up the pant legs of the jeans she found, she glanced around for a piece of rope to tie the big pants around her waist. Laughing she tied it around her. She knew she must look ridiculous, but she didn't care. She was warm and dry.

The overhead lights began to flicker and it scared her. She didn't like the dark. Looking around she searched for a lantern. There were always lanterns in the movies and in all the books, but there were none now.

Worried, she looked at the lights as they flickered again. She started ransacking the barn for a flashlight, but she couldn't find one. How could there be no flashlight out here? How asinine. There must be a flashlight! Frantically she searched and searched to no avail.

Feeling a panic attack come on, she tried to calm herself. The lights were still on she reasoned and she was safe and dry. Finally, she calmed herself. She started talking to the horses to relieve her tension.

Looking at her watch, she realized that she had been in the barn for hours and the storm showed no sign of letting up. Another vibrating boom followed by the crack of lightening sent her scurrying to an empty stall. The lights flickered again and went out.

The darkness made her tremble in fear. She feared the dark. Her stepfather would often lock her in a dark closet for hours at a time, after he beat her. This was a nightmare.

Curling up into a tight ball, Annie started crying, then sobbing. She couldn't seem to help herself. There was no way she could reason her way out of her fear this time. Not even the animals gave her comfort.

Running to the barn door, she decided that being out in the rain was better than being in the dark barn. She pulled on the door trying to open it. She tried repeatedly crying out with each try. She was locked in. She found it hard to breathe. Sliding down against the barn door, Annie put her face into her knees and held on.

What if the lightning lit the barn on fire? She wouldn't be able to get out! The animals would all die too. Try as she might she couldn't evict her dark thoughts.

The wind finally died down as the storm moved on. It gave her a small measure of relief that it was over, but the lights were still off. Gathering her courage, she stood and tried the door again. This time it opened. She ran across the yard to the house and tried the front door. It was unlocked too.

Tearing it open, Annie quickly entered the house. The electricity was off, but she could see a crackling fire in the family room. She moved closer and found Alice and Burke sitting on the couch enjoying the fire.

Burke looked surprised to see her. "I thought you were spending the night at Sherry's house."

"The doors were locked I couldn't get in."

"The doors at Sherry's?"

Annie ignored them and went to the fire to warm up. It boggled her mind that he was here in the house while she had been locked in the barn. "You didn't check on the animals?"

Shaking his head, Burke stood up. He walked closer to her and cupped her face in his warm hands. "What happened?"

The concern she saw in his face was too much for her to handle. She felt her legs give way under her. Thankfully, Burke was there to catch her. He sat in the chair closest to the fire and held her on his lap.

"Give me the blanket, Alice," he demanded.

"I'm using it."

"Damn it, Alice give me the blanket!"

"You don't have to get snippy with me." She threw the blanket at him.

"It's okay, Annie," he murmured, wrapping the blanket around her. "Can you tell me what happened?"

Shaking her head, she clung to him. He was her lifeline and she couldn't talk. She couldn't even cry anymore, she just clung to her husband.

Finally, she relaxed in his brawny arms, feeling safe. "The doors to the house were locked, so I went to the barn to get out of the storm. The lights went out so I tried to leave the barn, but that door was locked from the outside."

"I've got you. It's okay."

Annie sat up and looked at him. "No it's not okay! Why were the doors locked?"

"I was here the whole time and I didn't lock any doors. Besides you told me that you were spending the night at Sherry's," Alice said, sounding very believable. "I'll let you two sort it out, I'm going to bed." She took one of the flashlights and went to her room.

"We don't lock the doors here, honey."

"Just forget it! You never believe me anyway," she shouted, jumping up off his lap. "Does this look like my usual attire? I was soaked and cold. I found these clothes in the barn. The same barn that someone locked me in!"

"I don't think…"

"That's right don't think. I'm going to bed!"

"Annie."

It had been the most miserable night and now this. It was too much. Grabbing a flashlight, she raced to their room.

She stiffened when Burke later got into bed with her. Her took her into his loving arms and held her. "I believe you, Annie, I do. I'll look into it tomorrow, honey."

Annie sighed in relief and finally fell asleep.

The next morning, the loneliness was too much for her to stand any longer, so she went to the barn to watch her husband work. She was relieved to catch a glimpse of him. Standing in the doorway Annie watched his arm muscles bulge as he hefted a bale of hay. Her heart beat faster and her breathing became shallow. She was nervous approaching him after giving him the cold shoulder for about a week, but she loved him too much to let their discord go on any longer.

* * * *

He sensed her gaze, turned and looked at her. His eyes held hers. He was relieved to see her smiling at him. It'd been a hard week, trying to get close to her only to have her rebuff him. He smiled watching her blush. She suddenly looked like shy and innocent as she slowly approached him. He had to resist the urge to meet her halfway. It had to be her decision, her desire that made her come to him. Her rejection the past week had hurt him. He understood it, but it still hurt. He held his arms wide open and Annie ran into them, hugging him for all she was worth.

Burke grabbed her waist and lifted her up for a kiss. He was surprised and pleased by her passion. She couldn't seem to get enough of him as he felt her deepen each kiss. He felt her body trembling against his and he groaned. How he wanted this woman. His desire for her was unlike any other. He could barely contain his passion as he swung her up into his arms ready to climb up into the hayloft. He heard a noise behind him. Reluctantly he turned around to see who would dare to interrupt and wasn't surprised to find Alice standing there practically half-naked.

Burke held Annie close to him, his eyes narrowed on Alice's smiling face. "Did you need something?" he asked nonchalantly as if he didn't have a care in the world.

Alice pasted a false smile on her face. "I was just lonely and thought you might be in here," she replied in a sugary voice.

"I'm here as you can see, but at the moment you'll have to entertain yourself. My wife and I were just on our way to take a nap," he said casually, enjoying the hatred she spewed with her steel gray eyes. "Maybe you could use this time to make a few phone calls so you know where you'll be living by the end of the week," he suggested.

Annie giggled against Burke's neck. She held on to him tightly as he made his way across the yard to the house. He carried her up the stairs and gently placed her on their bed.

Burke slowly undressed her, kissing her all the while, eager to get her naked. He wanted her. It scared him just how much he wanted her. It wasn't the path he thought their marriage would take, but something inside him felt glad that his plan to keep his distance had somehow failed. He stared at Annie's body in rapt appreciation loving the silky softness of her skin. She looked so young, so beautiful, and so happy.

Her nipples hardened under his intense scrutiny. She nearly jumped off the bed when he rubbed her beaded nipples between his fingers. It felt like heaven. She tried to grab his head for a kiss, but he kept himself at arm's length, giving her a wolfish grin all the while. "Please," she pleaded in a taunt whisper.

Burke pushed both of her luscious breasts together and kissed both nipples at once, laving both with his tongue, making her cry out. He heard her plea and could feel her grabbing at his hair. He wasn't finished feeding off her, not yet. Looking up, he saw her green eyes filled with passion. He kissed her stomach, making her squirm and cry his name as he rained kisses lower until he found the exact spot he looked for. She shuddered and screamed holding tighter against him as she rode out her wave of pleasure. As she calmed a bit, Burke shucked his clothes and kissed his way up to her speechless lips.

"I don't want this to end too soon," he said, his husky voice straining.

"Why would that be?"

"I can't hold on much longer, if you keep touching me like that," he ground out.

Burke put her legs over his shoulders before he plunged into her. He was in her so deep it was pure heaven.

Burke thrust for all he was worth. She was made for him, he decided. He saw her eyes flare as she took her pleasure yet again. He groaned aloud and finally finished. It was hard getting his breathing back to normal afterward. Annie constantly amazed him with her willingness to try new things. Her passion was unequal to any other. Maybe city girls weren't so bad after all.

Burke smiled as he looked down at her. Her whole body was a rosy pink from their lovemaking and it made Burke proud that he was the cause. Her cheeks were red, her lips swollen, and she looked like a woman thoroughly loved. Her eyes were heavy lidded, so he knew she was ready to take that nap. He slowly got out of bed, so as not to wake her and got dressed. Ranch work never waited.

* * * *

Burke came home earlier than usual. "Where's Annie?" He asked Alice who was sitting at the kitchen table.

"I know you want to punish me," Alice whined. "I knew it before I got here, but for you to be so blatant about it is just plain cruel! Using that plain wife of yours to make me angry and sorry isn't fair. It's not fair to her or me. She must know how you still feel about me. I see it in your eyes every time you look at me," she cried.

"I'm married to Annie, not you."

"Tell me that you love her," she challenged. "Tell me and I'll go."

Burke turned from her and looked out the window. His silence was deafening.

It was especially so to Annie who stood at the kitchen door witnessing the whole conversation. Her face grew hot in humiliation as he refused to answer Alice. Her heart sank into her stomach.

She held her head up as she walked through the kitchen and grabbed her vegetable basket, not looking at either one of them as she slammed out the back door. She walked to the garden, knowing that Burke probably watched her. She refused to let him see her cry anymore. Hearing the backdoor slam, she expected Burke to come apologizing, but she heard the truck leaving instead.

Annie felt numb. Somehow, she had lost him to that witch inside. Her eyes filled with tears, but she quickly brushed them away. No more crying, she admonished herself. Enough was enough she finally knew the score. Now all she had to do was make a plan to leave. After her moving expenses, she only had about three thousand dollars to her name. She knew that she was a stronger person now than she was when she lived in the city. She could handle the future.

She quickly picked the vegetables she needed and walked toward the house with the painful knowledge that she and Sherry would not be canning them together. She was glad that Alice wasn't in the kitchen. Annie put down the basket and decided to take a hot shower wanting to remove all traces of Burke off her body. He repelled her. Somehow, he'd managed to make her feel dirty and ashamed.

Annie scrubbed and scrubbed, but she couldn't get the feel of him off her. Her skin was rubbed red when she finally got out and dried herself. She pulled on a pair of faded cutoff jeans and a teal T-shirt then walked to the stairs. She hesitated not knowing whom she'd encounter downstairs. She planned to make dinner and eat alone. Certainly, she wanted nothing further to do with either Burke or Alice. Their little game of punishment had cost her dearly leaving her feeling shattered inside. She knew that Burke had never said that he loved her, but she had somehow let her imagination run away from her.

She sighed. Once again, her instincts about men were terribly wrong. Burke had used her to get back at Alice. She felt so stupid, so pathetic.

Annie started down the stairs and suddenly she flew through the air to the floor below. She'd felt something trip her, but she didn't remember seeing anything on the stairs. Her pain intensified as she lay there and she knew that her leg was broken. Assessing the rest of the damage was out of the question since it hurt too much to move. She closed her eyes as her head began to throb and tried yelling a few times, but no one answered. She didn't remember seeing Alice before she went upstairs. Maybe she had left with Burke.

It seemed as though she was there for hours before she heard the back door slam. Her hair wet from her tears, she moaned pitifully. Cat had faithfully stayed by her side meowing in commiseration.

She didn't even have the energy to yell anymore, her voice had grown hoarse from her earlier attempts. She really didn't care who found her at this point.

* * * *

Burke saw the vegetables on the counter. He didn't see any dinner, though he didn't expect to. He was upset and ashamed by his fight with Alice, only because Annie had suffered for it. Why didn't he just didn't claim to love Annie? He thought that he did, but he couldn't seem to say it, not to his ex-wife. He should have gone after Annie realizing that she'd heard the whole conversation and would naturally leap to the conclusion that he didn't love her. Now he felt like a first class jerk. At the time, his need to get away had been so great that he had forsaken Annie.

Sitting at the table, he put his head in his hands. He didn't even know what to say to Annie and he felt sure that she wouldn't believe him at this point. He didn't want to lose her. He straightened as he heard a groan. Quickly he jumped to his feet, looking for the source. Finding Annie at the bottom of the stairs, he ran over, knelt down and kissed her forehead.

"Easy Annie, I'll call an ambulance. Just hang in there baby," he said as his heart twisted painfully.

Burke ran to the kitchen and called 911 requesting an ambulance. Just as quickly, he ran back to Annie to be by her side. He didn't like the look of her skin, ash white in some places and a splotchy red in other places. By the twist of her leg, he knew that it was broken. Her pitiful groans ate at him. If only he hadn't left.

"Burke," Annie whispered, in a hoarse voice. "Time," she managed to say.

"It's about six, honey," he replied. Cat looked at him with disdain.

"Two hours," Annie managed, looking at him.

"You've been here for two hours?"

Closing her eyes, she turned her head away.

"Annie, I'm so sorry." He brushed her wet hair away from her face with his fingers. Everything he did lately was wrong. It didn't matter what he did, he only ended up hurting her.

"Honey, I hear the sirens." He took her hand, afraid to let go.

Annie opened her eyes and stared at him. The pain she felt was evident in her expression, but it was the sadness that touched him the most.

Just as help arrived, she passed out.

* * * *

Waking was a painful process. Annie's eyes felt as dry as sand. She winced at the bright sunshine that flowed through the hospital window into her room. She was thirsty, so thirsty. Her throat hurt, in fact all of her hurt. She felt the splint on her right hand and tried to wiggle it, wincing. Her right wrist was sprained. She groaned, spotting the seemingly giant cast on her right leg. Annie heard someone clearing their throat and she slowly turned her head, not really wanting anyone to be there.

Burke stared at her. He looked like hell. She wondered why.

"Annie, do you know where you are?" he asked. "Do you know who I am?"

Annie took her left hand out of his large hand. "I know who you are," she croaked before she turned her head away from him. She couldn't deal with the wave of emotions she felt. She couldn't look at Burke and she certainly didn't want to talk to him.

A few days later, Annie smiled at her doctor as he declared her able enough to leave the hospital. She had been there for two days and she'd had enough of being constantly poked and prodded. She was still in a lot of pain, but anything was better than the hospital. Heck, she was even ready to put up with Burke and Alice while she recovered. She figured that Alice must be leaving any day and maybe, just maybe she and Burke could find a way to settle their differences. She wasn't sure if they could ever come together again. She harbored a lot of hurt and heartbreak, and she had a right to her feelings, but she felt bad every time Burke came to visit. He was often unshaved and he had circles under his eyes. He looked at her with big blue eyes full of remorse and pain. More often than not Annie had to turn away from him. She just didn't know if she could forgive the conversation she had heard between him and Alice. The pain that he didn't love her still felt too fresh, too raw for her to forget.

Annie planned to bide her time, get well and then weigh her options. She knew that she was strong enough to walk away if necessary. It would be painful, but she was already living an emotional nightmare.

She forced a smile as Burke entered her room. He carried a small bag of clothes for her in one hand and a single red rose in the other. Annie looked at the rose wistfully. She took it when he handed it to her. She could smell its full fragrance, and she wished that the rose had been given for its true meaning, love. Annie quietly thanked him not quite looking at him, but rather at a point just off to the side of his face.

* * * *

Burke knew that she was avoiding his gaze and he pretended that he didn't notice as he helped her into her clothes. He wanted to talk about their marriage. He wanted to tell her he was on her side. He wanted too much and she wasn't receptive to his conversations about them.

Every time he brought up the subject of their relationship, she shut down. She looked the other way and refused to answer him. It was pure agony knowing that he'd hurt her. He wished to hell that he'd just gone ahead and told Alice that he loved Annie. He just hoped it wasn't too late.

He talked to her about mundane happenings at the ranch, trying to lighten the mood by telling her all of the escapades of his ranch hands, Dan, Surly, Yates, and Nash. He did manage to get her to smile when he told her how they had started a fight with hands from another spread at the diner and Noreen managed to whack Yates in the head and Surly on the arm before she was done.

Annie almost laughed aloud before she reined herself in. "Are they okay?" she asked concerned.

"They'll live," Burke replied. "The real injury was to their pride. Dan and Nash won't let them forget it." He chuckled, happy that she was finally talking to him.

"What about Noreen?" she inquired.

"She proclaimed herself the hero in the whole thing."

Annie finally laughed. The tension shortly melted away altogether. "I don't know how I'll get around the next few days," she said ruefully as she gestured toward her sprained wrist and broken leg.

Burke took her hand in his and gave it a quick reassuring squeeze. "In sickness and in health," he said, not taking his eyes off hers. "I'll take care of you and it will be my pleasure."

The ride home from the hospital was silent, but to Burke's relief it wasn't uncomfortable. He had a feeling that Annie was going to need some time before she was accepting toward him and he prayed that he hadn't blown it for good. He was almost glad that she was in a cast and couldn't go anywhere else; he wanted her home where she belonged.

* * * *

Annie needed him, at least until she recovered. What would happen after that, she wasn't sure; it would be a wait and see kind of thing. She already knew that men couldn't be trusted and once again, lesson learned. She only hoped that this time the lesson stuck in her brain. She couldn't let her guard down again or allow her heart and emotions to make her decisions anymore. It just added up to heartbreak.

Annie smiled as she saw the ranch house come into view. She'd come to think of this place as her home. Her roses swayed in the light Texas breeze and it felt as though they were welcoming her. They were in full bloom and she looked forward to sitting on the front porch enjoying them. She waited in the truck for Burke to open her door. He was going to have to carry her in and she shivered slightly in anticipation. She knew that she would never let another man close to her again and she wanted to make memories that she could carry forever.

She stared at Burke as he lifted her from the truck seat into his arms. Annie put her arms around his neck and buried her face into his neck, loving the smell of him. He was all man with a scent of leather and spice. She closed her eyes, not wanting this moment to change.

Annie made a sound of protest when he finally put her down. Looking into his beautiful blue eyes, she saw raw desire. It gave her a start, but it gave her confidence as she realized that she had such power over him. He still wanted her, and it made her feel womanly and beautiful. She luxuriated in these feelings before she closed her eyes and tried to get comfortable on the couch. She waited until she heard him leave the room before she opened them again. She knew she had taken the coward's way out, but she couldn't think of anything to say to him. She needed to find her center first. Emotions were high and she needed to remember that she'd be leaving soon.

Annie was startled out of her musings by Alice waltzing into the family room with a tray of tea and sandwiches and a big old false smile. Annie would have been amused if she hadn't had some inkling that Alice was somehow responsible for her fall. Annie knew that she tripped on something and it wasn't her own feet. Alice was dangerous; she could just feel it. She had underestimated the woman before, but never again.

"So how is our little patient this afternoon?" she cheerfully asked.

Too cheerfully Annie felt. "I'll be laid up for a while," Annie began.

"And that is why I have volunteered to stay on and nurse you back to health," Alice jumped in.

Annie's eyes grew wide in horror. "I don't think that will be necessary," Annie insisted. "Let's just keep to your original schedule."

"It's really no problem. It's the least I can do," Alice said a bit panicky.

Burke grabbed a sandwich, acting totally ambivalent to the tension in the room. "I haven't eaten all day." He settled into his usual leather chair by the fireplace and began to eat. It didn't seem to take him long to realize that the other two women looked upset. He groaned as he asked the question. "What's wrong?"

Annie felt insulted that Burke seemed to ask the question of Alice and not of her. She remained quiet, waiting for Alice to offer her services. She didn't have long to wait as Alice began listing all the vast reasons and benefits to all of them if she stayed to help. Annie withdrew and shrank into herself. It was hard to see Burke watching Alice in rapt attention. Soon she stared out the window, trying to block them both out.

"Annie?" Burke prodded. "Annie, are you listening? This involves your life."

Annie turned her head to look at him, surprised that he wanted her input. "I want her out of my house," she simply said and turned her head away, not wanting to continue the conversation any longer.

"Alice, could you give us some privacy?" Burke asked.

Alice smiled. "Certainly," she said as she sashayed out of the room.

Burke waited until the screen door slammed before he spoke. "I'll have her out of here in three days."

"But," Annie tried to interrupt.

"Mrs. Harvy is unavailable until then and you can't be here all day by yourself," He said with disappointment in his eyes. "I know that Alice rubs you the wrong way."

"That's an understatement. Call Sherry." Annie responded.

Burke knelt in front of the couch, grabbing Annie's left hand. He kissed her palm making her tingle. "Ted and Sherry are out of town for a few days. I promise you, she will be leaving in three days."

Annie took his hand and rubbed the back of it against her cheek. "Let's just hope it's a quick three days," she conceded.

Burke smiled and gave her a quick kiss on the lips then stood up. "Get some rest. I'll be back in a few hours."

Annie nodded and yawned. "Good idea," she said with a slight smile. "By the way, where's Cat? I expected her to greet me."

Burke frowned. "I'm sure she's around. I'll look for her."

* * * *

Alice was shocked. She really didn't believe that Burke would actually kick her out. She shrieked, cried, begged, pleaded, and demanded, but Burke stood firm. He told her that she had three days and that was it. She felt panicky as she watched him march away from her. Her tearful pleading hadn't worked. It usually worked for the curvy blonde. She stamped her feet as she watched him get in his rusty old truck. She'd been so certain that causing Annie to fall would prolong her stay one way or the other. Now she wished she'd caused a fatal accident. Her eyes narrowed and her resolve firmed. She had a plan for her and Burke, a plan that involved millions of dollars, money that Annie didn't even know about.

Sonny had originally hired Alice to come back to Weltworth and make sure that the marriage didn't take place. They met when she had sold Sonny the piece of Burke's land she received in the divorce. After the sale, they had spent a nice long weekend together. They really did have a lot in common. They were both savvy in the ways of money. He was desperate to maintain control of Annie's money, trust fund money that Annie didn't even know about. She'd been too late to prevent the marriage, but she planned to break it up and marry Burke. His divorce settlement would be worth millions and she planned to get a portion of it for herself.

Alice calmed herself. Her goal was in sight and she wasn't going to let that little nothing ruin it for her. She smiled wickedly as she started to plan. They would never know what hit them by the time she finished. Alice patted her blonde hair in place and walked into the house. If they wanted her to be a nursemaid to that tramp, she would. She needed to keep her eye on the prize.

Chapter Eight

Annie felt a bit suspicious when Alice brought her a cup of tea. She anticipated having to wait for Burke to come home, but here was Alice being as pleasant as she could be. Something didn't feel right, but Annie accepted the tea gratefully.

"I'll be in the kitchen if you need anything," Alice said sweetly. "Why don't you take a nap? You look done in."

"I think I will, thanks," Annie responded hesitantly, eyeing the blonde beauty. "Have you seen, Cat?"

"No."

She didn't know what Alice's new game was, but she was too tired to worry about it. Drinking the tea, she thought it had an odd taste. "Alice!"

Alice looked into the room. "What now?" The impatience in her voice was grating.

"This tea tastes a bit off. What kind is it?"

"What do you mean what kind? You only have one kind, and that is what it is. I'm sorry if I can't even make a cup of tea to please you. You know, I'm beginning to wonder if the fall wasn't done as an attention getter." Alice's eyes narrowed. "I think you were jealous that Burke and I were getting cozy again, making a connection. You're pathetic and now you have the nerve to complain about the tea? Oh please, give it a rest!"

Alice's outburst astonished Annie. None of it made any sense. Alice was unbalanced. Annie felt suddenly very groggy. She heard Alice puttering around the kitchen as she fell asleep. She slept soundly.

Annie stretched her arms above her head trying to work out the stiffness from sleeping on the couch. In pain, she reached toward the coffee table for her medication and was surprised to see that it was gone. The table was empty. Her glass of water was also missing. Slowly, she sat herself up. "Alice," she called. "Alice, I need my meds and some water please." It killed her to have to say please to that witch, but she needed her.

Silence again greeted her. At first she thought that this was Alice's revenge for making her leave, but Annie was willing to give her the benefit of the doubt. She called for Alice two more times before giving up. The pain became unbearable and she urgently needed to empty her bladder. She couldn't stand it anymore; she had to get to the bathroom.

Gingerly she propped herself up to a standing position. It was very tricky with her right wrist and leg out of commission. Finally, she felt balanced enough that she took an awkward step toward the bathroom. She took one-step, then another before falling, face first onto the floor. Annie saw stars as she hit the wooden planks. If she had thought that the pain was bad before, it was substantially more so now. Annie swore as she felt her bladder relieve itself. Tears streamed down her face in pain and humiliation.

Just how long she lay there, she didn't know. It was unbearable to lie in her urine. She tried breathing exercises that she had read about to try to manage the pain. It didn't help much, but it gave her something to concentrate on. She worried about who was going to find her. Being helpless, she felt embarrassed. She tried to turn over and move away from the moistness but her pain was all-encompassing. She couldn't move.

Finally, there was a knock on the kitchen door. Annie heard Sherry calling out a hello.

"I'm in here."

Sherry walked into the family room and immediately got down on her knees brushing the wet, tear-plastered hair away from Annie's face. "Annie, can you hear me?" she asked. "Let me help you up," she offered.

"No!" Annie cried in panic. "Get my pain pills first."

Sherry hurried back with the pills and a glass of water. She helped Annie to move her head enough that she could swallow them. "Better?" She stroked Annie's auburn hair.

"I am, now that you're here, thank you." Annie reached out and squeezed her friend's hand in gratitude.

"How long have you been on the floor?" Sherry inquired. "Where is every one?"

"Burke's working and Alice was supposed to take care of me—"

"What?" her friend interrupted. Sherry was indignant. "Who allowed that to happen? My God the woman hates you, I just don't understand."

Annie gave Sherry a ghost of a smile. She gazed lovingly at her friend. Her only friend it seemed. Annie liked the way her brown eyes looked murderous, and it was all in defense of her. It had been a long time since anyone was on her side. It gave her a warm feeling, though it might have been the pain pills kicking in. "I think it would be okay to move me now, if you can."

"Let's do it slowly, one step at a time," Sherry suggested, gently rolling Annie onto her back.

Annie grunted and turned bright red. "I was on my way to the bathroom—" she started to explain.

Sherry squeezed her hand. "Accidents happen. Besides this wasn't your fault. Where is the witch from hell anyway?"

Sherry carefully lifted Annie to her feet, winding them both too much for anymore conversation. Slowly, Sherry helped her to the bathroom and cleaned her up. They laughed a time or two trying to get her clothes off and on over her cast. By the time they were done, Annie seemed to be in better spirits.

Step by slow step, they finally made it back to the couch. Annie sighed as she sank back into the soft cushions.

"I don't know how to thank you, Sherry. I'd still be on the floor if you hadn't stopped by."

"I'm just glad that I did come over. Ted and I were supposed to go to Oklahoma to visit his sister but he couldn't get away at the last minute. I'm still holding out hope for a small vacation. You never did say where your so called caretaker is."

Annie shrugged her shoulders. "I woke up to find my pills and water gone. I called out, but she wasn't here," she explained. "If she went somewhere, why take my pills away? It makes no sense to me."

"She probably did it to be spiteful," Sherry conjectured. "Burke told Ted that he gave her three days to get out."

"That's the plan," Annie agreed. "Mrs. Harvy should be back by then."

"Are you two country bumpkins gossiping about me again?" Alice asked cattily, making her entrance into the family room.

"Where have you been?" Sherry demanded. "I found Annie on the floor when I got here."

"Oops," Alice replied, putting her hand over her lips in fake dismay.

"Annie needed your help this afternoon."

Alice shrugged her shoulder as if she didn't care. "Like I said, 'oops.'"

"You are the sorriest example of a human being I've ever come across!" Sherry hissed. "Annie fell while you were gone and lay there for hours until I came along. Where were you?"

Alice barely blinked. "I was out." She picked up her packages. They were shopping bags from high-end stores. Annie and Sherry exchanged puzzled glances.

"What did you do, go all the way to Dallas to buy clothes?" Sherry asked in outrage.

Alice smiled at the brown-haired woman. "Where I go is none of your business. However, since you asked, a friend gave me money to spend. As you probably know, you can't buy anything decent around here." She smiled maliciously. She made an overt scene of studying the other two women's clothes. "Oh, I suppose you don't know that."

"By the way Alice, Where is Cat?" Sherry asked accusingly.

"Will you two give up on that damn cat?"

"Please, both of you just stop," Annie pleaded. "My head hurts from listening to you."

Sherry bent down and touched Annie's forehead checking for fever. "I don't want to leave you alone with her," she whispered.

Annie smiled. "Burke will be back in an hour," she gazed solemnly at Sherry. "Go, I'll be all right."

"If you're sure…"

"I'm fine now thanks to you." Annie gave her a weak smile. "I'll just lay here and before I know it Burke will be home."

Sherry hesitated finally she nodded to Annie. "Call me if you need me."

Annie reached up and hugged her. "I will, and thank you for helping me."

"I'm just glad that I stopped by when I did," she said as she gave Annie a quick hug back. "Take care."

"I will."

Annie made sure that Sherry had left before she turned a vicious stare at Alice. "You had no business leaving me like that," she cried. "Why did you take my pills and water away? I woke up in such pain that I got up by myself to use the bathroom and you weren't even here! I fell flat on my face."

"I'm here now," she said dismissively. She walked right past Annie and went upstairs with her many packages.

Annie wondered where she had gotten the money to shop in such expensive places. She'd made it known that she was broke. Alice was up to no good, that much Annie knew to be true, but just what Alice was up to she didn't know.

"Annie." Alice came back down the stairs. "I have something I think you should see. I cleaned Burke's office and I found these papers, dated a few weeks ago. It's addressed to you and already opened."

"Here I think you should read it yourself." She handed the letter to Annie. "I couldn't for the life of me think of a reason that Burke kept this from you."

Annie wasn't in the mood for any of Alice's phony concern, but she took the letter from her. It was addressed to her and the return address was that of her mother's lawyer, Charlie Banks. Her fingers trembled slightly as she opened the letter and began to read. Her heart beat faster as she realized that she was a woman with quite a bit of money. She closed her eyes remembering her stepfather always calling her *his duty, his obligation, his waste of money*. He would beat her for it, and the money had been hers to inherit on her wedding day. Tears fell down her face as she remembered Sonny calling her nothing but a millstone around his neck. She also remembered how he would hit her. She nearly laughed as she recalled him saying that she was nothing more than a poor relation that he should kick to the curb.

She grew deathly white and wanted nothing more than to run into the bathroom and get sick, but she didn't have that choice. She wouldn't be running anywhere for quite a while. She really couldn't wrap her mind around just how much she was worth. It was in the millions. Then her heart twisted looking at Alice who said that she had found it in Burke's office. Annie looked at the date of the postmark and it was indeed weeks old. Burke had kept this from her and she had no idea why. "Why didn't Burke tell me?"

"I don't know. He never said a word to me. I know that he's been having money problems and he might even lose the ranch. Maybe he didn't want you to know that he married you for your money. Maybe he was going to wait a while, when you were too in love with him for it to matter."

Annie was heartsick. "We signed a prenup," she said shakily. "It was his idea."

"Who wrote up the prenup?" Alice asked.

Annie closed her eyes. She didn't want Alice to see her downfall. "It was Ted," she replied bitterly.

"Did you read it?" Alice prodded.

"No, not the second one. I only read one page of it. The page I wanted changed." Annie shook her head at her own stupidity.

"Maybe he has a perfectly good explanation," Alice offered.

Annie shook her head. Her shoulders slumped in defeat. "I can't think of one," she said sadly. "If you don't mind, I'd like to be alone."

"Of course, I understand. I'll just go to bed."

Annie nodded absently. Her mind was on other matters. She couldn't believe what her life had been like since her mother's death. She wondered what role Alice played in all this, since she always had an angle and she certainly hadn't told Annie out of the goodness of her heart.

The worst was Burke's part. Whatever his position was, he had lied to her. He had deliberately kept her mail from her and he had the nerve to open it. The only conclusion she could come to was that Burke already knew what was in the letter. Alice was probably right, he married her for her money, money that she didn't even know she had. He hadn't even told her how bad his finances were. He never mentioned losing the ranch. She knew that they were tightening their belts to get through until he sold his cattle, but why did he tell Alice and not her? She was his wife. They were supposed to share their problems. Being married for her money was humiliating. He certainly played his part to the hilt. He got his wish; she was very much in love with her husband.

She didn't know what to do. She really needed to stay until her leg was a bit better. Already the pain in her wrist was lessening and Annie became determined to try out her crutches tomorrow.

Annie dozed on and off all night and never heard Burke come in, but he had left his Stetson on the coffee table, so she knew that he was home. She was still very troubled by everything she had learned. Looking above to the balcony, she had a perfect view of each room. All the doors looked closed and she almost closed her eyes again, but she suddenly heard laughter. Her senses honed to Burke's door and she was surprised to see Alice sneaking out wearing a see-through yellow teddy, smiling as she tiptoed to her own room.

Rage slammed Annie back to her pillow. She wished that she could run up those stairs and give them both a piece of her mind. How dare they? They must have known that there was the possibility that she would see Alice running around half-naked. She felt so helpless.

Her first instinct was to confront them both in the morning, but she really wanted to know what they were planning. Maybe she was jumping to conclusions. She felt deep in her heart that Burke was not the type to cheat on her. However, lately the honesty and integrity that had attracted her to him seemed to be false. Tomorrow she would call her mother's lawyer and find out the details of her inheritance.

Sighing heavily, she buried her face in her hands. She felt her foundation slip away. She no longer had anything or anyone to hang onto. Her whole life seemed like a gigantic lie, one big fat lie. Annie clenched her fists and pounded silently on the couch. What was it about her that made everyone feel as though they could take advantage of her?

Annie was so angry. She was angry with her mother, her stepfather, and her stepbrother. She was livid at Burke and his role in all of this. However, most of all she was angry with herself for being so stupid, so naive, so... She couldn't think of anymore words to call herself. It shamed her that she gave her trust and love so easily. Everyone must have thought she was desperate for attention, for affection, for love. How humiliating to know the truth. Most people would be thrilled to discover that they were suddenly very wealthy, but it was a small consolation prize as far as Annie was concerned.

Pathetic was the word for it, she thought. But they always said that what didn't break you made you stronger. She reached out and grabbed onto that ideal. It would become her mantra. Right now, she needed a backbone and thicker skin.

The next day went painfully slow. Somehow, Annie wasn't surprised that she didn't lay eyes on her husband all morning. She'd been waiting for a return phone call from Charlie Banks and it made her restless. Alice had been somewhat pleasant to her all day. It made Annie sick to her stomach just to look at her. She glanced at her crutches leaning against the coffee table. The sooner she got better, she thought as she reached for them, the sooner she could take back her life. It took a bit of finagling and practice, but she finally got it down. The pain was still there, but maybe the pain would make her stronger too. It definitely made her more determined to be independent.

Tomorrow was supposed to be the big day. Alice was supposed to leave. Annie wondered what would really happen. She really didn't think that Alice would leave, but she was anxious to see how it all played out. It amused her to wonder what lies they would feed her this time.

Annie painstakingly circled the room again, aware that Burke watched her.

"Wow great job!" Burke praised. "Why don't we go sit on the porch and get some fresh air?"

Annie gave him a quick glance and then looked away. "No thanks," She made her way to the couch. She gingerly seated herself and promptly ignored him.

"We could sit here and talk if you'd like."

Annie wouldn't look at him. She stared down at her wringing hands. She couldn't seem to still them. "No I would rather be alone." She didn't want to talk to him, he just had to accept it, for now.

"Day's a-wastin," he said as he left'

Watching him leave left a bad feeling in the pit of her stomach. How dare he pretend to be concerned?

The phone rang and Annie waited for Alice to answer it. Instead she heard a familiar voice on the answering machine.

Struggling to get up, she picked then picked up the phone and began to dial.

Annie hung up the phone after her talk with Charlie Banks. He had been trying to get a hold of her for the last few weeks but he'd been told that she was unavailable. She had her suspicions about that. The amount she stood to inherit was staggering. She was worth over forty million, more if Sonny hadn't been siphoning off some all these years. Her resentment toward him and her stepfather knew no bounds. Annie really didn't care so much about the money, but that didn't change the fact that they had been stealing from her while making her believe she was worthless. The most interesting part of the conversation was that Burke had never contacted him about the inheritance. She puzzled over for most of the afternoon, but she just didn't know what to make of it.

She was getting around on her own now and it felt great not being dependent on Alice for her every need. She even was so bold as to ask Alice where she would be going tomorrow when she moved out. To Annie's pleasure, Alice sputtered and stomped out of the room. She was finally getting a backbone, and she liked it.

All night, Annie had her eyes glued to the closed doors on the upper floor. Tonight she planned to confront them. She had a feeling that last night had been set up by Alice just for her benefit. She felt sleepy, but was determined to stay up and watch the doors. She prayed that Alice would not go to Burke again. She didn't know what she would do if that were the case.

A pang of regret went through her. Burke had looked so tired and groggy before he'd finally gone upstairs. She couldn't bring herself to talk to him.

She started to doze, and then she heard a door open. Looking up. she could see Alice in a sexy red number tiptoeing to Burke's room. Annie held her breath willing the woman to keep going toward the bathroom, but that didn't happen. Her heart lodged in her throat when Alice opened Burke's door and snuck in.

Annie couldn't leave it there; she had to see for herself. She knew that Alice was capable of such actions, but Burke? Now was not the time to give him the benefit of the doubt. It was time for facts. She groaned as she swung her legs off the couch. The stairs loomed large, but she didn't have a choice. She had to climb them. She had to know. The doubts had been eating at her for too long.

She loved him, and she had found a self-worth here in Texas that she hadn't possessed before. She deserved the truth and she deserved a faithful husband.

Step by painstaking step, Annie climbed the stairs. Her brow grew wet with sweat and her breathing became labored. Finally, she reached the top, and she felt so winded that she had to take a break. Her stomach was in knots. Filled with dread, Annie opened Burke's bedroom door.

She couldn't contain her cry of despair when she saw Alice on top of her husband. Burke didn't even look up at her, but Alice smiled at her over her shoulder. They were both naked as Alice bounced up and down on Burke. Annie gripped the doorjamb for support, afraid that she would fall. She finally forced herself to look away and leave the room.

In shock, she climbed back down the stairs, sat down at the kitchen table and stared into space. Until she had seen the evidence, Annie had held on to the smallest of hope that it was all a bad dream, but she realized that she could no longer hide her head in the sand. What a fool she had been. Now she needed to get out of there fast. She didn't want either of them to see how much they had hurt her.

She thought of calling Sherry but didn't want to get her involved just in case Ted was part of some plan to defraud her. Suddenly she thought of Noreen. There must be someone at the diner that could give her a ride to the airport for a fee. She looked at the clock and was surprised to see that it was only nine. Her hand shook as she picked up the phone and dialed.

"You poor dear," Noreen commiserated. "Don't worry sugar your secret is safe with me. I'll just say you have a family emergency. Hold on a sec."

Annie could hear talking in the background before Noreen picked the phone up again. "Hank is here, as usual, and he'd be delighted to take you to the airport."

"I don't know how to thank you, Noreen. You've been a good friend."

"You keep your chin up kid and don't be a stranger," Noreen said before she hung up.

Annie began to get herself ready to go. She was still half waiting for Burke to come downstairs and beg her to stay, but she knew deep down that it wouldn't happen. Still, that was her, forever hopeful. Thank goodness that a good amount of her clothing had been bought downstairs when she broke her leg. She put as much as she could in a shopping bag, grabbing her purse and crutches. She wanted to be on the front porch by the time Hank arrived to take her to the airport.

She sat on the front porch of the house that had embraced her and filled her head and heart with promises.

Burke did too, she thought as her heart twisted painfully in her chest. The wind had kicked up a bit, a warm wind, making the roses sway back and forth. At one time, she would have been fanciful and would have thought they were greeting her, but now she knew differently. If anything, they were calling her a fool, waving good-bye, giving her the old heave ho.

She was thankful when she saw the headlights of Hank's truck bouncing up and down the lane. She was starting to question her sanity. Roses were just roses and houses were just houses. Most importantly, you only had yourself to rely on. You only had yourself to blame. Her heart did ache for Cat, but she knew that she was gone for good.

She gave Hank a quick smile as she climbed into his truck with her shopping bag and crutches. She was glad that he didn't seem inclined to talk. When they arrived at the airport, he helped her down and tugged on the brim of his cowboy hat, giving her a sad smile and walking away.

Chapter Nine

It had taken five weeks, but Annie now had the evidence she needed to confront Sonny. With the help of her lawyer, Charlie Banks, she was now in sole control of her inheritance. She also had many of the forged documents she planned to use to confront Sonny. It sickened her how he'd treated her while he helped himself to her money.

Rumor had it that he was spending a lot of time with her one-time friend Lisa. Rumor also had it that they were playing house in her old apartment. She hadn't known it, but she owned it. Armed with her evidence, Annie felt stronger than she ever had. Her cast had finally come off and she felt fine. No one was going to ride roughshod over her again. She was her own woman now and she was on a mission.

She glanced at herself in her compact mirror as she rode to her old address. Money had its privileges such as a car and driver. She had her hair done, her nails manicured and a complete makeover. Who knew that she'd been a diamond in the rough? She hardly recognized the beautifully turned out confident woman staring back at her in the mirror.

Annie looked forward to their little meeting. In fact, Sonny was unaware that she was even in town and she couldn't wait to see his face when he learned that she knew of his deceit. Too bad his father wasn't still alive to feel her wrath too. She pasted a serene smile on her face when her driver opened her door. With her spine stiff and strong, she entered the building. She waved to the doorman, who tried to intercept her.

"Miss Douglas," he called as she headed for the elevators. "Miss Douglas you don't live here anymore."

Annie coolly turned around. "Excuse me?"

"Your stepbrother advised me that you were not to enter the premises again," he explained apologetically.

Annie smiled. "Don't worry, Frank. You won't get in trouble. In fact, I'm still grateful for all your help a few months ago, but my stepbrother doesn't own the apartment. I do." Annie gladly showed Frank the necessary paperwork.

Frank chuckled. "I have a feeling there's going to be some fireworks around here soon."

Annie laughed with him. "You better believe it."

Frank pushed the elevator button for her and shook his head as the doors closed.

Annie's heart began to race at the thought of confronting her stepbrother. She smoothed down her high-powered Gucci suit, fixed her heavy gold jewelry, and patted her professionally styled hair. Looking at her long nails she practically laughed aloud. She looked more like Alice than Alice did now. After the meeting, all that was fake would wash away. She didn't like this style and never would, but she had hoped to shock and intimidate Sonny with her new look and her new determination. After all, she had all the cards and wasn't about to back down. This wasn't only for her and all the years they had treated her like a dog. It was also for the baby she suspected she carried. The thought of being pregnant thrilled Annie, but her emotions toward Burke were still too raw. She had always wanted to have children, a family. Now she would be a single mother, but she wasn't daunted. She knew that she had what it took to do a great job.

Annie snapped out of her musing as the elevator door opened into the penthouse apartment. She had always wondered why she lived in such a nice place. Sonny just said that it was an investment. Now she knew the truth; it belonged to her.

Sonny and Lisa both jumped up as they heard the elevator open. Annie relished in both the shock and the looks of recognition on their faces. She wanted to laugh at them but kept a cool, indifferent facade. She knew that she couldn't show any sign of weakness for Sonny to prey on.

Sonny wore his usual tailor made suit, with his black hair slicked. He thought it was in vogue, but it just made him look greasy. His dark eyes simmered with rage.

Lisa looked worse for the wear. It was obvious that she wasn't taking care of herself. She was usually so perfectly made up with her chestnut hair curled and bright eye shadow highlighting her golden eyes. Now she looked weary and haggard. Annie wondered if the tinge of blue on her chin was a bruise.

Annie sashayed into the living room, the same way she had watched Alice make an entrance. "Please, don't look so surprised," she admonished softly. Annie made an overt gesture of walking around the apartment, touching her own things that she had left behind. "The place still looks good," she remarked offhandedly, ignoring both their stares.

Finally, she turned and looked Sonny straight in the eye. He tried to stare her down, but she refused to cower as she did in the past. She smiled at him as he glared at her. "We have some business to attend to dear, dear, Stepbrother," she almost purred. "I've been to see Charlie Banks."

She walked to the windows that spanned one whole wall. She had always loved the view from here. She took it all in, fortifying herself before turning toward Sonny with narrowed eyes. "You remember Charlie don't you?"

Sonny's face turned pale. "I don't know what line of bull Charlie has been feeding you, but he's wrong," he sputtered.

Annie almost laughed, but she kept her cool facade. "I think not. In fact I have document after document, files and more files of your crimes against me."

Sonny took a step toward her, wanting to intimidate her. He reached out and grabbed her upper arm in a vice-like grip. "Think again. I do what I want." He grabbed her arm tighter and yanked her toward him. "I'm still in charge."

Annie pulled her arm out of his punishing grip. She could feel the bruises forming, but she knew that she had to remain calm. Shaking inside, she pretended to examine her newly manicured nails, needing a moment to regroup. "So you're with Lisa now?"

Sonny laughed. "I always was, baby. I set you up with Jeffrey so that you would never get married. He's gay, actually, but was willing to play along for the right price."

Annie's eyes widened. Turning, she stared at Lisa. "But I saw you in bed together," she protested.

Lisa laughed long and hard, making Annie feel small. "It was all a set up. Honestly, Annie you were ripe for the picking. Who could possibly want you? My God, you're as cold and dumb as they come."

"The past is over," Annie declared, straightening again. "I have business to discuss with you Sonny and I believe that you'll want to hear the deal I'm willing to offer you." Annie opened her bag and flung a huge file on the glass coffee table. "Read them and weep," she retorted.

Sonny grabbed the file and flipped through it. He groaned and sank down hard onto the white couch. His shoulders slumped in defeat.

He ran his fingers through his black hair. "What's this deal you're talking about?"

Annie was surprised just how fast the fight went out of him. "According to my accountants you have taken over twenty million dollars from my trust." She turned as she heard Lisa gasp. "Don't worry I seem to have plenty more."

Annie turned her attention back to Sonny. "Here are my conditions," she began. "I want the Texas property in my name, I want you out of this apartment, and most important, I never want to see you or hear from you ever again."

Sonny studied her for a minute. "No jail? No authorities?"

"Right, just sign the property over to me and move out, it's that simple."

Sonny grabbed the pen that she had held out to him and signed the deed immediately. He threw the pen down on the table. "I'm going to be ruined. All the money is gone.".

Annie serenely picked up the signed papers and put them along with the thick file into her bag. She walked toward the elevator and turned. Cocking her head, she looked at Sonny. "You know, you've been nothing but a millstone around my neck and it kills me that I had to spend any money on you at all," she said, repeating the oh-so-familiar taunt. "I want you out of here by the end of the month." She stepped into the elevator. "Oh, and Lisa? You are such a bitch."

* * * *

Six weeks later Annie sat overlooking Central Park, waiting for her architect to show up. She felt impatient to get on with her plans. Two more weeks and she was heading home to Texas. She missed Weltworth and the people she had come to know. Smiling to herself, she looked down at her faded jeans and green T-shirt. She didn't need expensive clothes or things for that matter. It felt good to be independent, but she missed Burke. She knew that their marriage was over, but she couldn't help but remember the good times.

Annie jumped when the doorbell rang and she quickly answered it and let her architect, Van Crawford in. She was glad to see him. They had been working together for almost six weeks now, remodeling, rebuilding, and outfitting her property in Texas. She was paying him a fortune, but he was worth it. He understood how important it was to her to maintain the integrity of the original house while adding on and upgrading it.

Annie led Van over to a table by the window where they could go over the plans. She was building a horse ranch and she was so excited about the whole project. She smiled at Van. No matter how many times she saw him, she couldn't get over just how good-looking he was. He had whiskey-colored eyes that often winked at her. His blond hair looked rich and thick and he filled out a T-shirt nicely. He was so beefy. Unfortunately, her heart remained occupied. She had no room for anyone else except for the little one growing inside her. She unconsciously touched her lower abdomen and smiled. Van smiled back at her.

Annie looked over the plans for the barn. "I'm a fish out of water as far as the barn is concerned," she admitted. "We're going to have to hire someone experienced in horse breeding, training, hell I don't know a damn thing about horses." She laughed.

"I think I have a solution to that," Van remarked. "I've been spending a fair amount of time in Weltworth and I happen to know a guy we can hire."

Annie's eyebrows raised in question. She knew from experience that the grapevine in Weltworth ran fast. "Well?"

"I found out that a man named Clint Maloney just had his ranch foreclosed on. I hear he's the best around with horses and knows about cattle as well."

"If he's so good why did he go into foreclosure?" Annie asked.

"I don't know the whole story, but his wife died—"

"Say no more," Annie jumped in. "If they have nowhere to go offer him the job."

"He has a daughter too."

"Then tell him a house comes with the position. If it turns out he can't handle it we'll just get someone else, but I want him have a home."

"Gathering strays are you?" Van asked, chuckling.

"Why do you say that?"

"You already hired Mrs. Harvy to be your live-in help. I heard that she had only one month's rent left in the bank. Then there is Jimmy McKeegan. Heck, you've never met the guy, but because he's Noreen's cousin you hire him and build one of the nicest bunkhouses I've ever seen."

"I know what it's like to feel unwanted and to have nowhere to go."

"Annie, you've got a big heart."

"Find this Clint fellow and offer him the job," she instructed. "If he has nowhere to go right now move him and his daughter into my new bedroom. That should give them enough room until their house is built. Have him go over the plans for the barn and we'll use his expertise."

Annie walked Van to the door. "Oh, one more thing, check with Noreen. She will know the 411 on this guy, but either way, give him a place to live at my house for now." Annie hugged Van. "I'll be there in two weeks," she said happily.

* * * *

Annie had chosen a window seat on the plane since she wanted to see Texas from the air. She was going home finally to a place that was all hers. And she didn't have to depend on anyone's goodwill or fickle heart anymore. She'd spoken to Van yesterday and he said he'd have someone there to meet her, driving her brand new Texas pickup truck—cherry red of course. Practically bouncing in her seat, she waited impatiently for the cabin door to open when they landed.

Finally, she stood at the luggage claim. She looked around trying to spot a familiar face, but she saw none. Instead, she found herself standing in front of the most rugged man she had ever seen. His face was very angular with laugh lines deeply etched into his skin. He was very tan as though he spent most of his time outdoors and when he took off his hat to greet her she could see his midnight black hair. It was curly, but he kept it cut short.

"Mrs. Dawson?" the man asked.

"Annie—just call me Annie," she immediately said. She didn't like using her married name. "You must be Mr. Maloney." She spotted a little girl peering up at her from behind her father's legs.

"I'm Clint ma'am," he said with a touch of shyness.

Annie didn't think he was a shy man. Maybe around women, but he had the look of a Man's man, just like Burke. She stopped her thoughts from going there. She didn't want to think about him, at least not today. "Nice to meet you Clint," she replied as she crouched down. "Who is this beautiful princess?" she asked with a smile.

The girl was adorable. She peeked out from behind her father's legs and smiled at Annie. "Are you a princess too?" she asked in awe.

Annie laughed. "All girls are princesses at some time or another. What's your name?"

"Ennie," she said in delight.

Clint laughed and reached down to sweep his daughter up into his strong arms. "That's right sweetheart, your name is Rheenie."

A leg brace on the little girl's leg was prevalent and it tore at Annie's heart. She could see the love between them and was immediately envious.

After locating her luggage, they were off. Clint wasn't much of a talker, but his daughter made up for his lack of verbiage. Annie loved looking at Rheenie. Her hair was black like her father and she wore it long and straight, secured by a black velvet headband. Her brown eyes shone with excitement and her face was so animated that Annie was immediately smitten.

"My daddy said to thank you for a roof," she said very seriously.

Annie looked over Rheenie's head at Clint for clarification. He had already translated many things for Annie. "She means a roof over her head," he chuckled. "Seriously though, Annie, we are beholden."

"I feel like the lucky one here." Her heart swelled. "I need your experience and knowledge. I'm just happy that you took the job, and this little one is definitely a bonus."

"She's something, all right." He laughed proudly.

"Annie, I'm a princess, not a smothin'," Rheenie explained, patting Annie on the face with lollypop-sticky hands.

Annie took her hands and kissed them, "I know you are, baby, I know."

As soon as her house came into view, Annie asked Clint to stop the truck. She wanted to take it all in slowly. The house was magnificent. It still had the old farmhouse look mixed with freshness. It had been painted butter cream yellow with emerald green accents. The front porch looked lovely repaired and painted white. She loved it. The rose bushes were pruned, but they were still there as well. It wouldn't be long before they bloomed again.

Annie opened the truck door. "I want to walk to it alone," she said to Clint.

Clint nodded and drove up past the house toward the bunkhouse.

Annie approached her house in awe, feeling the pull of it. It was the same magical feeling she'd felt when she had first come here. Was it only months ago? Annie felt she'd grown years since then. Closing her eyes, she took in the sounds of the birds and building. She laughed; yes, she heard and smelled building. The smell of sawdust was very prevalent. It was a smell of new beginnings. She looked up at the big blue Texas sky and asked God to let this place be her haven.

Touching the screen door, Annie smiled more. It was the original, repaired, but the original. Anticipation welled up in her, wondering what other surprises she would find. The family room had the original wood floors, although refinished. The huge rock fireplace looked to be in working order and Annie was thrilled that the scarred wooden mantle was still in place. It was everything she imagined and more. The furniture had been reupholstered, and one Queen Anne style chair had a beautiful hand-sewn tapestry on it. Van had mentioned the needlework he found in the attic. Annie gently ran her fingers over the fabric. She was home, and this time she knew it was right.

The rest of the house was a delight as well. The kitchen still had the original counter tops, scars and all. The big farmhouse sink was still there, modernized by new fixtures. It all blended in and gave the room an overall look of the early 1900s.

Mrs. Harvy's room was off the kitchen. She had requested that room, and it was lovely. Peeking into the spare room, she was surprised to see that Clint and Rheenie's things were inside. She had told Van to give them the master bedroom since it was bigger. Making a mental note to ask them about it later, Annie moved on.

Finally, she made her way to her room. It was huge. She gasped as she saw the bed covering. It was lush and opulent, covered in throw pillows and it sported a pattern of roses. Her bathroom was also decorated with a rose motif. She looked at her garden tub and instantly knew that it would get a lot of use.

Hearing a sound, Annie went back to her room. There stood Mrs. Harvy with a great big smile on her face. "Beautiful isn't it?"

Annie quickly hugged the other woman. "Did you—?"

"No," Mrs. Harvy answered quickly. "Van picked it all out. Not only is he a great architect, but he knows how to restore furniture and he likes to decorate. He has great taste."

Annie wholly agreed. Van had outdone himself.

Mrs. Harvy seemed to sense Annie's need to be alone. "I'll go make us some tea while you take this all in."

"Yes," Annie agreed absently. She opened the French doors that led out to the porch. She wanted to cry she was so happy. When she felt the tears on her cheeks, she blamed them on hormones.

"Don't be sad."

Annie looked down at Rheenie and smiled. "I'm not sad, I'm happy," she explained.

"Tears, sad," Rheenie said shaking her head at Annie.

Annie sat in one of the wonderful porch rocking chairs and lifted Rheenie onto her lap. She loved the feel of the little girl so close to her. She wondered if her baby was a boy or girl. Either way she'd be happy. Annie kissed the top of the little girl's head. "I'm not crying anymore. You make me happy."

"I don't make people happy. People are always sad with me," she said then sighed. "Mostly my daddy."

Annie's heart lurched in her chest. She cuddled the child even more. "I'm sure that's not true. I bet he's very glad to have you."

"You bet I am," Clint agreed with a smile, coming out to join them, you two look like you're getting along just fine."

Annie smiled back at him. She could see the sadness and pain in his eyes. He tried to hide it, but now she realized why Rheenie thought she made him sad. She hoped that this place would be a place of healing for all of them. "How's the barn building going?"

"These guys are fast and efficient," Clint said. "Van has really designed a state of the art breeding facility."

"Yes, he is good. He said you did most of the work though."

Clint looked glad that she was pleased. "All we need is some thoroughbreds with good blood lines and we're good to go. I've already found a stallion that would be a big moneymaker. I'm going to have to be quick on my feet, but I think we can buy him. There is a horse auction in Fort Worth this Saturday if you'd like to go."

"I'll leave the buying to you, but I'd love to go and Rheenie can join us."

Rheenie jumped out of Annie's lap and jumped into her father's arms. He lifted her up and she squealed, "Rheenie go! Rheenie go!"

Clint hugged her tight. "Yes you can go, but right now Mrs. Harvy said she has milk and cookies for you." He looked over the top of his daughter's head. "I believe that Mrs. Harvy also mentioned something about tea for you."

"Sounds good."

* * * *

Annie had never seen so many horses in her life, or so many cowboys and she just loved it. Wearing her new red cowboy boots and her tan Stetson, she felt a part of things. She looked down at Rheenie who wore a pink cowgirl outfit that Annie had bought her. She was as cute as a button. She didn't wear boots because of her leg brace and special shoes she had to wear. Annie was very conscious of the stares that Rheenie got. She felt outraged on the girl's behalf, but she knew that there wasn't a thing she could do about it.

They made their way up the bleachers and sat next to Clint, who instantly picked Rheenie up and gathered her on his lap. Annie had noticed how much attention he gave to his daughter and it made her glad. Clint already looked through the catalog and had inspected the horses on which he planned to place a bid. Ironically, most of the horses he wanted used to belong to him, before the foreclosure. They had discussed the budget before leaving the house, and Annie was willing to pay top dollar. She wanted her dream of a horse ranch to come true.

Annie scanned the crowd, enjoying people watching, especially the families. She envied them, but she knew her time was coming. Looking straight across the arena, she was shocked to see Burke staring right at her. Her heart began to beat faster and she almost forgot to breathe. She hadn't expected to see him so soon. In fact, she had been keeping close to home just to avoid him. She needed to tell him about the baby and she needed to do it soon. He looked good, handsome as ever. His brown hair could have used a trim, but somehow it made him look sexy. Her heart felt like it was in a vice and she began to tremble. She bit her lip so hard that she drew blood, yet she couldn't look away. Clint asked her if she was okay, she turned to look at him and nodded. When she turned back, Burke was gone. Annie frantically searched the large crowd for him, but it was useless.

Annie tried to put up a good front for the rest of the day, but her mind kept going back to Burke. God help her, but she still wanted him. She was glad that Rheenie was there. She filled in all the silent gaps with her enthusiasm, managing to make Annie laugh a few times. But all the while Annie could feel her heart breaking all over again.

Chapter Ten

Annie heard through the local grapevine that Burke was in danger of losing his ranch. His divorce settlement with Alice had wiped him out and he was never able to regain his footing. It made Annie sick to know that he might lose it all. She knew how much the land meant to him. She had called his house and left messages, but he never called back. She wanted to tell him about the baby and to ask him about the divorce. She still hadn't received any papers. Finally, she left a message telling him that he was to become a father, but she never received a reply to that either.

At first, she thought that maybe he wasn't getting his messages. Alice probably erased them. Certainly, he would have contacted her about the baby. Annie finally decided to drive over to his house to confront him directly. She was almost four months pregnant and she knew that she would be showing soon. That trip to the maternity store was getting closer and closer.

Annie was disappointed as she drove up to his house and saw that his truck was gone. As soon as she stepped down out of her truck, Alice was right in front of her. Her angry look almost frightened Annie.

"What the hell are you doing here?" Alice demanded.

Annie looked at her perfect hair, her perfect nails, and designer clothes and wanted to laugh. "I guess you don't do much housework in those clothes."

"Unlike you, Burke doesn't want me to be his housekeeper," she retorted.

Annie sighed. She had a feeling that things were going to get nasty. "Have you been deleting my messages to Burke?"

Alice laughed. "No! He's listened to each and every one of them. He even mentioned how pathetic you were."

Annie stood her ground. She wanted to leave and never come back, but she had promised Burke that she wouldn't keep his children from him. "He knows about the baby then?"

"Oh, you mean the baby that's not his? Yes, he knows all about it and wants no part of it. In fact we're going to get remarried," she said, her voice filled with malice.

Annie was stunned. "He doesn't think the baby is his?"

"I think you heard me the first time. He knows what a whore you are. You're not passing off another man's baby on him, honey. He's too smart for that."

Annie felt the color drain from her face. She held her hands together to hide the trembling. "The marriage?" she asked softly.

"Does the word divorce mean anything to you?" Alice smiled triumphantly.

Annie turned and got back into her truck. She didn't know what she had expected, but it certainly wasn't this. How could he believe that the baby wasn't his? She was heartsick. She got halfway home before she had to pull over. She took a few tissues out of her purse and had herself a good cry. He thought she was a whore.

In all honestly, a part of her had been happy to see him at the stock show. She didn't want to admit it, but there was still hope in her heart. At least… there was. She hated that she still stupidly loved him. He wasn't hers anymore. She cried out her grief for quite a while before she pulled together. She didn't want anyone at home to know she'd been crying, but she knew that there was no way to hide her red eyes. Luck was with her, however, since somehow she managed to get home and into her room without bumping into anyone.

Her mind whirled and whirled. She found it all so hard to believe that she needed to hear it from Burke himself. She couldn't accept it until he told her. With shaking hands, Annie called Burke's house again. She was hesitant when he answered the phone. "Did Alice tell you that I was there today?"

"She told me everything," he said angrily. "Don't call here again and don't come here again. We are through. Do you understand?"

"Yes," she choked out. "I understand perfectly." She hung up the phone feeling numb, finally realizing she was on her own. She was going to be a single mother. Her child would never know its father. It was so crazy that Annie couldn't comprehend it.

How did it all come to this?

She thought of a paternity test and of demanding child support, but in the end, she realized that if Burke married Alice, then Alice would be her child's stepmother. There was no way she'd allow Alice to have access to her baby, no matter what.

As much as she wanted to lie in bed and tune out the rest of the world, she told herself to buck up. There was her horse ranch to build, a legacy to her child. She pressed a wet washcloth against her swollen eyes. It served Burke right to lose his land, she decided spitefully. But as she calmed down, she realized that Burke's land was also her baby's legacy and she wasn't going to let it go to strangers.

Maybe she could buy the ranch from him, so he'd have something to live on. In the end, she decided to pay off his mortgage and his debts. Though there was a part of her that felt bitter, she planned to go to the bank tomorrow. Feeling a bit better, she went to sleep.

* * * *

After her cup of coffee the next morning, Annie was off. She wanted to get to the bank early. She had a lot of business to take care of.

Mr. Todd the bank manager was happy to see her. She had deposited a large amount of money when she first arrived back in Weltworth.

The amount owed on the mortgage was staggering, but Annie didn't blink an eye. It must have been a tremendous burden for Burke to carry. She deposited twenty-five thousand into his account to cover everything.

Feeling better about things, Annie thanked Mr. Todd and left his office. As she walked toward the bank door, Burke came in. Immediately she lowered her head, unable to look at him as she tried to pass by. Burke blocked her way and glowered at her. "I meant what I said last night; I don't want to see you." Annie hastily nodded, and quickly sidestepped him, hurrying out the door.

She could still see the anger in his eyes as she walked half a block to the community garden. She had never been there before, but it looked inviting after the bank episode. It was deserted and

Annie sat down on the wooden bench. The garden contained not only vegetables, but also an abundance of different flowers. She smiled as she recognized the vegetables, thanks to Sherry. The flowers had her guessing since she wasn't very familiar with the different varieties. It was already getting hot even though it was still morning. Unfortunately, sitting in the garden didn't give her the relief she hoped for, so needing to find some sort of comfort, she walked across the street to Noreen's diner. She knew it was a mistake as soon as she saw Burke sitting at the counter. Noreen greeted her warmly and Annie tried to smile but couldn't.

"Damn it!" Burke roared. "Are you stalking me now? I know what you did at the bank and I'm sorry, sweetheart, but I'm not for sale not at any price, especially not to you. So, paying off my debts didn't buy me back. I don't know how many times I have to tell you that I don't want you. Stop following me, stop calling me, just leave me alone!"

Annie slapped him in the face. The violent action shocked her, but she wasn't sorry. She turned and ran out of the diner. She could hear Noreen calling to her, but she couldn't stop. Right now, she needed to be as far away from Burke as she could get.

* * * *

Noreen stood in front of Burke. "You bastard. How could you yell at that little gal like that? I am so ashamed of you! You aren't the only one she has helped with her money. Yes, helped not bought. She paid off this place for me and she gave Mrs. Harvy a home and started a retirement account for her. She took in Clint and his little Rheenie when they were homeless. Even old Rowdy has a few new trucks in his rental fleet."

Noreen looked like she was going to explode. "She's done nothing but give to this community! She's donated to the church and the schools. Why she even gave my nephew Jimmy a place to live and work. She has employed most of this town for one thing or another, now especially when times have been so hard. That bitch Alice has you all turned around again! Annie didn't want to buy you. She wanted to give you the one thing you wanted most in the world, your ranch free and clear. And don't tell me that it doesn't mean anything because I happen to know that you were a month away from foreclosure!"

Burke was astonished. He couldn't believe what he was hearing. He hadn't kept up with the Weltworth grapevine, so he didn't know how generous Annie had been to those she cared about. She'd been generous to the whole community and he had yelled at her for it. He felt like a fool, a complete fool. "I'm sorry," he mumbled to Noreen, leaving the diner with his head low.

He sat in his truck staring at the steering wheel, thinking what a fool he was. How could he have yelled at Annie that way? Ever since he'd seen her at the horse show with Clint and his little girl, he had been looking for a fight. He'd felt gut kicked seeing her with another man. When he mentioned it to Alice, she told him that they had been living together for a while. She had led him to believe that they were "together." Now he had a lot of thinking to do. He hit the steering wheel with his fist. He needed to get on his horse and ride until he dropped.

Driving home Burke's heart felt as though it was twisting inside him. He felt as though he had been gut punched and kicked around the yard. Now he had serious doubts about what Alice had been telling him. Why hadn't he given Annie the benefit of the doubt? She was his wife, for crying out loud! Was she still his wife or had the divorce gone through? He couldn't get his head on right. He pulled his truck up in front of the barn, saddled his favorite horse, and took off as though the devil was after him.

* * * *

Annie sat rocking on her front porch with Rheenie on her lap. Rheenie had become a balm to her heart. At least she had closure. Burke said he didn't want her, now she finally believed him. Her brain had known for a while, but finally her heart knew it too. It was almost unbearable. She felt as though she was mourning a death and perhaps she was. She was mourning her first and only love.

She looked down at the precious girl sleeping on her lap and sighed. In so many ways, she was blessed. She knew that. She just wished that she could concentrate on the positive instead of a dead relationship. Since she was carrying his baby, she thought of Burke constantly. She almost laughed aloud at the ridiculousness of the situation. She just couldn't believe that a man who still felt responsible for his ex-wife had no problem denying his own child. What happened to the integrity she had so admired?

Out the window when I saw them in bed together, she reminded herself.

Maybe she shouldn't have paid off his debts. She probably hurt his big male ego, but there was no way she could stand by and let his place fall into foreclosure. She had no regrets doing that. Hopefully someday he would see it as an act of kindness. For now, she had a baby to bring into the world and a ranch to build.

Clint walked over softly, bent over, and kissed his sleeping daughter on the forehead. "Want me to take her?" he whispered.

Annie shook her head no. She needed the closeness right now. Clint nodded back with a grin and walked toward the barn. She wondered about him. There was sadness in his eyes that never seemed to go away.

Annie's eyes followed Clint to the barn, where watched him talk to Van. They were going over the plans for the barn, although it was practically finished. She admired both of them. Maybe if things were different or if she had met either one of them first, before Burke... Speculation was foolish. She had enough to do without making herself crazy with what ifs.

Clint's house was almost finished and Annie was feeling a bit sad that Rheenie wouldn't be living with her anymore. It had been a week since she had last seen Burke, but as always he was on her mind. She hadn't called her friend Sherry since she'd come back to town because she didn't want to put her between herself and Burke. Finally, she decided enough was enough. She missed her friend and she needed someone to talk to. Sherry didn't have to pick sides. As far as Annie felt there were no sides, not any more. She'd faced up to her reality.

Sherry sounded thrilled to hear from her. The reunion between friends was full of hugs and tears.

"I can't believe how much you've done. This place is great. So when is the little one due?"

"Talk about the elephant in the room," Annie laughed, "I'm almost six months."

"Does Burke know?"

"Yeah, he does," Annie said, her voice full of sadness. Annie's face lost its glow and her eyes filled with sorrow. "He says it's not his."

"You've got to be kidding me?" Sherry demanded. "What universe does he live in?"

Annie gave her a sad smile. "If you could have Ted send me a copy of the divorce papers I'd appreciate it. I need a copy of the prenup too."

"Ted didn't take care of the divorce," Sherry informed her. "We don't know who he used, but I'll have Ted get you a copy of both items. I just don't know what Burke's problem is. He needs his head examined. What he really needs to do is get rid of that blonde snake."

Annie sighed. "It is what it is. I have spent whole nights lying in bed wondering why he denies this child is his. I have no answers. A DNA test could prove it to him, but I'm not going to bother. It's his loss." Annie looked out at her land and smiled. "I'm going to raise this little one alone, but I have tons of support. The people living here on the ranch have become like family to me and of course I know that I can always count on you." Annie smiled at Sherry and she took her hand. "I don't want to ruin your friendship with Burke. I know that you and Ted mean the world to him. He doesn't let many people close to him."

Sherry squeezed her friend's hand in reassurance. "It'll be hard not to give him the stink eye from time to time, but I'll try," Sherry teased.

"See you soon?" Annie asked.

Sherry hugged her and was startled to feel the baby kick. "I'll be around, you can bet on that."

Annie watched Sherry drive away and felt much better about things. She didn't have any power over Burke's actions and she had to let that go. There were times she thought that maybe she had, but inevitably, some small thing would remind her of his smile or his touch.

Smiling, she watched Clint take time out of his busy day to push Rheenie on the tire swing. The more she saw him the more she wished that she knew what his story was. She wasn't going to pry. She was just glad to have him for a friend.

Later that evening Annie received a call from Ted. He told her that he hadn't handled the divorce and couldn't find it filed anywhere. As for the prenup, her money was definitely still her money. He did say that he had talked to Burke about the divorce and Burke didn't even know the name of the lawyer. Alice had offered to take care of it for him. Ted also told her that it looked like they were still married, but Burke was going to confront Alice about it in the morning.

Annie thanked Ted for all of his efforts and gently hung up the phone. She was puzzled, deeply puzzled. Burke didn't marry her for her money or it would have been in the prenup, and shockingly there was no trace of the divorce papers. Alice had even told her that she and Burke planned to remarry. Something was fishy. It didn't make any sense, but with Alice, it never did. Annie shook her head as she realized that she had been foolish to let Burke handle the divorce. Hopefully she would have some hard answers tomorrow.

If he hadn't handled it, she would have to. Everything was turned upside down with Alice the one constant, and if he didn't see it then the hell with him. He didn't deserve to be in their lives. What she needed was a good swift kick. Allowing her thoughts to go there was foolish. It only added up to heartache.

* * * *

Burke was confused when he got off the phone with Ted. Annie had been on the level. She wanted no part of his ranch. Somehow she'd inherited a large amount of money and was benevolently giving it out to those in need right here in Weltworth. He was glad to know that Mrs. Harvy was going to be taken care of. He would have offered himself, but he really thought that he would be homeless in another month or so. The price of beef had gone down and his profit margin was gone. He should have thanked Annie instead of humiliating her and yelling at her. Ever since she had left him, for no apparent reason, he'd painted her with the wrong brush.

When she'd left, he was so angry. He worked from sunup to sundown and then some trying to tire himself out each day so that he could sleep. The more he thought about her the more bitter he became. He had this done to him once before, by Alice. He'd waited for some word from her, thinking that she would at least want alimony. What a fool he had been. She was worth millions.

What surprised him the most was that she had come back to Weltworth to live. She could live anywhere in the world, but here she was. He wondered why. In the back of his mind, he secretly had wished it was because of him, but now he knew better. Burke cocked his head as he heard Alice walking around in her bedroom above. He hoped she wasn't going to try to seduce him yet again. He had already told her that he'd never touch her—ever. Sometimes she pouted and sometimes she gave him a secret little smile as though he didn't know the whole story. He didn't care. He hardly saw her, working long hours. But now he wondered what her part in all this was. She said she'd take care of the divorce and at the time, he was too hurt and angry to think straight. Ted mentioned that the divorce wasn't on file, but Alice had told him that he was divorced. He really hoped now that he wasn't. As hurt as he was by Annie's leaving, he realized something. He still loved her.

Sure, he'd been enraged when Alice left. He felt used and had taken a huge blow to his ego. This time, Annie leaving him was different. He missed her constantly and felt as though half of him was gone.

He heard Alice's high heels clicking on the wood floor in her room. He shook his head. Who in their right mind wears high heels at a ranch? Annie wore jeans and T-shirts. She'd wanted to work the ranch. She had wanted to be a partner with him. Why did she leave? She never even said good-bye, and that ate at him constantly.

Glancing at the phone, he wished he had the balls to call her. He needed to apologize to her, but he didn't know what to say. She probably wouldn't talk to him anyway. He knew that he deserved her anger; maybe time would make a difference. Maybe he could avoid her. Burke ran his hand through his thick brown hair and sighed heavily. Knowing that she was living so close to him was both comfort and torture. It was a relief to know where she was, but it was hell not seeing her. It was so hard knowing that she lived just on the other side of his fence and wouldn't welcome him.

He'd confront Alice in the morning about the divorce papers. Something just wasn't right and he wanted to hear her explanation as to why the papers were never filed. With heavy heart, Burke went to bed, though he knew it would be yet another sleepless night.

* * * *

Alice looked surprised to see Burke sitting at the kitchen table drinking coffee. She hadn't gotten up early since Annie had left and he was usually gone by the time she woke.

She waltzed into the kitchen smiling at Burke. "Good morning, darling!" she rang out cheerfully.

"We need to talk," he said simply.

"Of course, darling," she drawled. "Anything you want, you know that," she purred suggestively, giving him a come-hither look.

"I talked to Ted. I wanted a copy of the divorce papers."

"You know I didn't use Ted."

"Well, *darling*, it seems that he can't find the papers on file anywhere."

"Oh that." She shrugged her shoulders. "I'm sure that it's a clerical error somewhere."

"I want a copy of the papers."

"I don't know why you want to bother yourself with such distasteful things. But if it'll make you feel like a free man, I have a copy in the study. I'm surprised that you didn't see them."

Burke's eyes narrowed as he looked at her. How he'd ever found her lovely was beyond him. She was ugly inside and out. He knew that she had to be lying. He'd spent every evening going over the ranch books trying to find a way to save it. Surely, he'd have noticed the divorce papers if they were there.

If it hadn't been so important, Burke would have laughed. Why hadn't he seen right through her to begin with? She was making a nuisance of herself and he really didn't even like her.

"Maybe you can go get them for me," he challenged.

Alice seemed unaffected by his tone. To his surprise, she calmly left the room only to return shortly with a manila envelope in her hand.

"Here you go, Burke." She handed the envelope over to him. "I don't know how you could have doubted me," she pouted.

Burke didn't even answer her. He immediately opened the envelope and looked at the papers. He'd seen similar papers before and these looked about the same, just what he expected. Maybe it was just a clerical error. He'd call Ted later. Work still had to be done, and all this waiting around for Alice to get up had been trying.

Burke shoved the papers back into the envelope. So it was over. He was divorced from Annie. He felt her loss keenly. He got up, grabbed his Stetson and walked out the door, letting the screen door slam loudly.

"Day's a wastin'," he said to himself miserably. Thank God, he still had his ranch to give him solace. Hard work would get him through. He did need to talk to Alice about her leaving, but that could wait. He just didn't have the energy it would take to get her to leave. He got in his truck and slammed his hand against the steering wheel, but it didn't help to ease the wound to his heart. He drove off hoping to work himself hard enough that he could forget the woman on the other side of the fence.

* * * *

Burke ran into Ted a few days later and told him that he did have the divorce papers. Ted asked Burke to get the name of the lawyer that handled the divorce. The decree had to be on file for it to be legal, so he offered to look into it again once Burke gave him the lawyer's name.

Burke had felt a bit uncomfortable with his childhood friend. He knew that he wasn't pleased with the way his marriage had fallen apart, but Burke had a feeling it was more than that. He had probably heard about his row with Annie at the diner. Hell everyone seemed to know about it. In fact, this was the first time he had come into town since then. He needed to place an order for horse feed.

As awkward as it was, Burke was glad to see Ted. He thought about their friendship as he drove home, and he knew that the uncomfortable feeling would go away. After all Ted was still looking out for him as far as the divorce was concerned. Burke dismissed it as his thoughts turned to whose money he had used to buy the feed. He was now grateful for Annie's gift.

He couldn't get her off his mind and it made him crazy. He was still bitter that she had left him. He had thought that everything was going well. She seemed a little standoffish after her fall, but he blamed it on the pain she was feeling. Something didn't add up, but he'd be damned if he knew what it was.

He drove his truck to the edge of his ranch and stared out at Annie's land. He could make out her house, a barn and it looked like another house on the property. He admired what she had accomplished. If rumors were true, she was on her way to having one of the top horse ranches around. Gazing longingly at the other property, he wished that he had the right to go on it and knock on Annie's front door, but he knew that he wouldn't be welcome. His heart felt heavy, filled with sadness. Turning his truck around, he made his way home.

Chapter Eleven

Annie snapped out of her melancholy for a moment. She hadn't even heard Mrs. Harvy come out of the house. She gave her a watered down smile. "I'm fine," she answered automatically, not wanting to focus on how she felt. She still felt like she was mourning a death and she couldn't help it.

"All this moping around really isn't good for the baby, you know."

Annie smiled at her housekeeper and friend. "I know. You're right." She took in a deep breath of fresh country air and straightened up in her chair as she caressed her protruding stomach.

"Why don't you go and catch that new movie in town?" Mrs. Harvy suggested. "I don't remember the name, but I heard that it's really funny."

Annie hesitated. Going into town really didn't appeal to her, but Mrs. Harvy was right. She needed to stop all her moping. Going to a comedy might be just the thing to shake her out of her present blues. "Thanks," she said as she awkwardly got out of the rocking chair. Annie kissed Mrs. Harvy on the cheek. "I think I'll do that."

Mrs. Harvy smiled in return. "It'll do you good."

Annie was rethinking her decision as she crossed the town limit. Maybe this wasn't such a good idea after all. Maybe she should have invited Mrs. Harvy along. No. She'd gone to movies alone before. She'd gone to Broadway plays alone, so she could do this. After all, she deserved to have some fun.

Annie parked her car on the street and walked over to the theater. It surprised her to see a line forming in front of the box office. Smiling, she nodded to people she knew. She really wasn't in the mood to socialize; they were obviously looking at her belly. She had finally bought maternity clothes and was surprised to find that the current trend was shirts that clung to the belly instead of shirts that tented the stomach. There was no hiding her pregnancy.

She had nothing to ashamed of. Her baby was conceived in a marriage and at the time, it was conceived in love.

Thankfully no one tried to engage her in conversation. She felt a bit self-conscious, but she really was looking forward to the escape the movie could give her.

A cool breeze kicked up as the sun began to set. Fall was one of her favorite times of year and she was looking forward to harvesting her fall garden. Sherry promised to come over next week to help her.

Annie glanced at her watch. The person running the box office was a bit late. She shifted from one foot to the other, waiting. Then she heard someone behind her talking. "I heard she was back after up and leaving Burke. She certainly has put on the pounds." Annie heard a familiar voice say. It was the same voice she had heard in the diner comparing her to Alice.

Annie felt her face grow red as everyone looked at her. Annie couldn't stand the pitying looks anymore and turned to walk away. Surprised to see Burke she glanced at him, but walked away.

She almost tripped stepping off the curb. Hands reached out to steady her and she was both surprised and relieved to see Ted. All he had to do was whisper her name and she fell into his arms enjoying his hug.

Ted smoothed her back as he whispered encouraging words to her. She pulled away from him and gave him a contrite smile. "I'm sorry; I don't know what came over me."

"I'll drive you home," he offered.

Annie gave him a weary smile. "Thanks, Ted, but enough is enough with that man and his girlfriend. I need to buck up and not be so sensitive. I'm so blessed with the people in my life and that's all I need remember."

Both Alice and Burke were walking toward them. Ted turned both he and Annie away and started toward his car.

Burke grabbed Ted's arm trying to get him to stop. He stood in front of Annie and looked at her very pregnant body. His eyes grew wide she could feel them on her big belly and her lush breasts.

"Go away, Burke," Annie said dully, not even bothering to look at him. She tried to walk around him. She knew that she was in no condition to spar with him.

Burke angled his body so that she couldn't pass him. "My God! You're pregnant!"

Annie almost laughed. "Yes, you've known that for months now." She finally looked at him and saw his confusion. She didn't know what to believe. It was probably some act for all those who were still staring at them. It seemed that a lot of them had foregone the movie in place of reality. "I need to go home."

Ted put a protective arm around her shoulder and stared Burke down. "Now's not the time, Burke. Buddy, from what I've heard you denied that the baby was yours."

Burke backed away from Annie, not taking his eyes from her face. "I didn't know," he insisted, staring at Annie. "I didn't know."

Annie made no response. She turned her head into Ted's shoulder and let him lead her to her car. She was so silent that Ted was worried. "You okay to drive?"

"Good night, Ted, thank you," she said as she gingerly climbed into the truck.

Once she arrived at her home, her haven, she saw Mrs. Harvy rushing toward her and she put a hand up. "I just want to be left alone, please, I need to think."

Mrs. Harvy reluctantly nodded and gave Annie her space.

Annie thought that as soon as she closed her bedroom door that she'd have a meltdown, but instead she sat on her bed dry eyed and frustrated. Either Burke was a great actor, or he really didn't know. Arguments could be made for either. The picture of him in bed with Alice flashed before her and she decided that her well-being came first, no matter what. She had to grow up, face reality and put Burke behind her. She needed positive thinking. She wanted to evict the negative thoughts, for good.

Annie caressed her stomach as she thought of all she had accomplished. She had a wonderful home, her horse ranch was more than a reality than a dream. She had surrounded herself with people she could love and depend on. She had done this, not Sonny, not Burke, not some other man she had clung to. No, she did it. It was her accomplishment and she should feel proud of herself. Annie finally smiled a real smile. It had been a long time coming, but she finally felt good about herself. Whether or not Burke knew about the baby really didn't matter anymore.

She was taking her pain and frustrations from the past and the present and giving them up to God, grasping on to a new wonderful future. Her baby was going to be a major part and it was already bringing her joy. In her sorrow she had been denying herself joy. Not anymore. She was loved, she was happy, and she deserved to be able to enjoy her blessings.

For the first time in months, Annie slept peacefully.

* * * *

Burke drove like a maniac. Seeing Annie pregnant had really upset him. He gave Alice a sidelong glance. Something was stinking to high heaven and he was positive that it was Alice. He couldn't wait to get her home and interrogate her. He wasn't going to put up with her bullshit or any of her pleading and crying. He was going to get the truth and he was going to get it tonight. His heart twisted painfully as he remembered Ted saying that he had denied that the child was his. How? Why? Parking the truck haphazardly. he quickly got out. He couldn't wait to hear what Alice had to say. On the other hand, she followed Burke inside, acting as though nothing was wrong.

"Too bad we didn't get to see the movie," she said petulantly.

Burke's eyes almost bugged out of his head. "After everything that went on tonight, you're sorry about not seeing the movie?" he asked in disgust. Burke stared sightlessly at the stone fireplace wondering where to start. What a mess and it was his mess. He should have never allowed her back into his life.

He turned toward Alice, pinning her into her chair with his angry glare. "How about we talk about this baby I didn't know about but apparently denied?" he demanded, almost growling.

Alice licked her lips nervously. "I was just trying to protect you, darling. I don't believe that the baby is yours. Annie is a whore; you need to face up to it," she said flippantly.

Burke took a step toward Alice, his fists clenched tightly at his sides. "How dare you call Annie a whore? How dare you! She was a virgin when I married her for God's sake."

"How was I supposed to know that? After all, she takes off, goes to New York and comes back pregnant? I was watching your back."

Burke's eyes narrowed. "How did you know where she went?"

She looked nervous. "I just know."

"I'm going to find out all of your lies sooner or later so you might as well spill them."

Alice took a step back. "She kept calling and leaving messages for you and I erased them. Then she came out here to announce her pregnancy and I told her that you already knew and that you thought that she was a whore and the baby wasn't yours," she explained as if she had done him a huge favor.

"Why?" he shouted. "Why would you do something like that?"

Alice pursed her lips together, trying to look so sorry. "Because I love you, Burke. I didn't want her to come between us." She tried pouting, she tried batting her eyelashes, and she tried cocking her head to the side and looking contrite.

"Get this through your thick head. There is no US! Do you understand me?" he roared, boring his hate-filled eyes into hers.

Alice got up and ran up the stairs, pretending to be weeping hysterically.

Burke had caught that particular show before, too many times.

He ran his trembling fingers though his brown hair. He felt like such a fool. How could he have been so stupid, so blind? There would be no talking to her now. Her moods were legendary. Tomorrow would have to suffice.

The whiskey flowed easily into his glass. It went down nice and smooth. Why? How? He couldn't wrap his mind around what happened in town. A baby, his baby. Hell, he was divorced and his ex-wife was having his baby.

A jackass, plain and simple, that's what he was. A stupid, gullible, jackass. He tossed back two more shots of whiskey and decided to call it a night. He suddenly felt bone weary.

The next day, Burke spent the morning moving the cattle to another pasture. Alice usually slept late and he wanted her wide-awake when she gave him her answers. He had a bad feeling in the pit of his stomach that there was more to it than he was seeing.

He turned his horse and rode for home. He couldn't stand not knowing any longer. Alice was in the thick of it he just knew it.

Approaching his barn, he saw one of Old Rowdy's rental trucks in his driveway. It looked to be the same one that Annie had the day he met her. He thought that Noreen said that Old Rowdy had a new fleet of rentals because of Annie.

Swinging down from the saddle, he led his horse to the corral. He briskly unsaddled him and took the bit and bridle off. "I'll be back to give you a good brushing in a bit, boy."

A scream came from the barn and his first instinct was to run toward it. He stopped himself and walked silently to the door. Alice was holding her cheek and talking to a man whose back was turned.

The man turned a bit and Burke could see the Glock pistol in his hand.

"Sonny, I told you I'm sorry. I tried every which way to break them up."

"You stupid cow, you were supposed to make sure they never got married in the first place. But no you were too busy taking a Hawaiian vacation with my money!"

"I... I got here as soon as I could honest."

Sonny lifted his hand, threatening her with the gun.

"You won't shoot me."

Burke wanted to put tape over Alice's mouth. He had to get to his rifle in his truck.

"You're right, I'm not going to shoot you. I just wanted to come see you and give you a little what for. You cost me everything!"

"Please, Sonny, I can still get Burke to marry me, and then I'll be in control of his half of Annie's trust fund. Don't you see baby? I'm doing it all for us."

Burke slipped behind the barn, used his cellphone to call the Sheriff, and hoped that he wouldn't be seen making a run for his truck. He heard Alice scream again and off he went racing across the yard to his truck. Ducking down he made it to the driver's door and opened it, reaching under the seat to grab his rifle. He cocked it and ducked down again, waiting to make another run for it toward the barn.

"After I'm done with you, I'm going to see that bitch sister of mine. A minor but fatal accident will take care of all my problems.

So you see, I don't need you." He aimed the gun at Alice while she screamed.

Burke got into position just in time and shot the gun right out of Sonny's hand. The gun went flying and Sonny cried out in pain. He whirled around, looking startled to see Burke. The blood poured bright red down his arm. "What are you doing here?" He turned and looked at Alice. "You said he was out of town."

Alice still had her hand on her cheek. "Guess I lied. Sorry."

"You shot me." He looked at his bleeding hand and then back at Burke, and quickly dove for his gun that was on the ground.

Burke kicked the gun further away. With his rifle aimed at Sonny, he leaned down and retrieved the gun.

"Thank God you got here just in time, Burke. You always come to my rescue."

Taking a step back he looked at Alice with disgust. "Stay right where you are, Alice. I know you are up to your neck in this."

"You can see what a monster he is, Burke. Just let me go. You can pretend I was never here."

"I wish I could pretend, but I can't look the other way for you."

"Hold it right there!"

Burke was relieved to see Sheriff Bodin standing in the doorway.

"Burke, drop the weapon." Burke nodded and put his rifle on the ground.

Sheriff Bodin put handcuffs on Sonny, who whined the whole time.

"What in tarnation is going on around here? Alice is that you? I heard you were back in town. You should have stayed gone."

Alice stepped forward. Tears poured down her face and she still clutched her cheek. "He hit me, Sheriff. Arrest him."

Sheriff Bodin shook his head. "I'll be the one who decides who goes to jail. Now sit your skinny little ass on that hay bale over there." He pointed to the hay bale near the first stall.

"I don't even know this man. He just showed up with his gun and he hit me. I've been terrified the whole time."

The sheriff rolled his eyes. "Burke, what's the deal with these two?"

"I don't really know. It has something about the money Annie recently came into. From what I understand, these two planned to take it from her. That is Sonny, Annie's stepbrother. I do know that he beat her up before we were married. He threatened to kill her."

"Kill her?" The sheriff stared at Sonny.

Alice stood up. "He said he would cause an accident to be sure that Annie's money went back to him."

The sheriff shook his head. "Burke, do you want me to take Alice in too?"

It was tempting, almost too tempting. "No, I need to talk to Alice about some shenanigans that have been going on around here."

"I'll take this dirt bag in and I'll be back out to make sure that Alice hasn't committed any crimes." He gave Alice a hard look. "You'd better cooperate with Burke. He holds the key to your jail cell."

Alice gasped. "But—"

"Save it Alice. I never did like you." He grabbed Sonny's arm. "A quick stop at the Doc's office and then off to jail.

"Now wait a minute. I'm not going anywhere."

Burke wanted to laugh at Sonny. How the hell did Annie survive having to live under his rules? His heart hurt just thinking about Annie. He needed the whole story from Alice, and then hopefully he could have a talk with Annie.

"See you in a few, Burke, and, Alice, so help me if you give Burke a hard time, I'll put your skinny ass in jail too for just being a public nuisance."

Alice sidled up next to Burke. It made him cringe to have her so close but he knew the score. Everything was all about Alice. She never thought of anyone else but herself. The best way to get her to talk was to make her believe that it was all about her.

They watched as the sheriff put a ranting Sonny into the back seat of the police car. Burke turned and looked at Alice. To his surprise, she looked rather pleased with herself. "Come on, let's go inside and you can tell me all about it."

Alice nodded. "He hurt my cheek you know."

"I'll get you some ice. Go on into the family room." Burke watched her leave and took a deep breath. All he wanted was to throw Alice off his property, but he needed answers. He took the time to make coffee, trying to regain his sanity. He wrapped some ice in a cloth and brought it to Alice.

"Thank you."

"Okay, out with it." He put the coffee pot and two mugs on the table.

Alice smiled. "I was originally supposed to make sure that you and Annie never got married. Since I was too late for that, Sonny wanted your marriage broken up. Sonny stupidly thought that he could legally take back control of Annie's trust fund if she was divorced. I decided to cut Sonny out and made a little plan of my own."

"I wanted to scare her away. She seemed like such a little mouse that I figured I'd give her a good scare, and she'd be gone. I set the trap in the hayloft, and I told her that there were little bitty kittens up there," she said, chuckling.

"How'd you get the trap set?"

"I just took it off the wall. It was already open and set. The fact that you were convinced that I couldn't have done it was a big plus. Actually, it was fun watching you and Nash running in circles, doubting the men you work with. It took the heat off me," she boasted.

Burke groaned, rubbing his hand over his face. He needed to portray an outward calm or she'd clam up.

"I wanted to make her jealous, so I played up to you constantly. I wanted her to feel lacking as a woman. It wasn't hard with that little nobody you married. Burke, you used to have such good taste."

"Sonny told you about her scarred back," Burke murmured. He had wondered about it at the time. With each sentence, Burke became more disgusted by the way she bragged. Her face grew more animated with each confession.

"One of my best ones was the night of the storm. You were supposed to be away, remember, darling?"

Burke simply nodded, bracing himself.

"I locked her out while you were away. It was storming something awful. One of the worst I've seen before. I saw her run into the barn and I put on your rain gear and slipped the bar on the door locking it. I heard her crying, trying to get out. I waited a few and unlocked it, but I guess she didn't try it again until later. By that time, you and I were cozying up by the fire. If not for her, we could have had made passionate sex in front of the fire place."

"I never suspected you."

"I know! I'm that good!" she said smiling brightly. Alice got up and poured herself a cup of coffee. "Want some, Burke?"

Burke shook his head. The way she said his name was like fingernails on a blackboard. He wanted to squeeze her neck until she quit breathing.

"A special delivery came for her from her lawyer and I opened it and hid it. That part had been Sonny's idea. He hoped that she wouldn't find out about the trust fund at all. But I realized that if I could convince her that you married her for her money, it would make her doubt you."

"Well, it obviously worked," Burke replied bitterly.

Alice smiled. "Oh no, even then she wasn't convinced that you were a cad. I had to come up with an even better plan. It was such fun planning the next part. It wasn't until she found us in bed together—"

Burke shot out of his chair. He couldn't contain his building anger anymore. "We were never in bed together," he ground out. "I didn't cheat on my wife."

Alice went on, taunting him. "I had to make sure that you couldn't sleep together, so she had a little fall. It was quite easily accomplished with a few nails and a bit of fishing line. It was brilliant, actually."

"Damn you!" Burke shouted, as he remembered the pain Annie had been in when he had found her at the bottom of the stairs. "You could have killed her!"

"That would have made everything easier. Since she didn't die, I drugged you and I made sure she saw me going into your room. She didn't come up the first night."

"There was more than one night?" he asked incredulously.

"Oh honey, it wasn't until the second night that we were together. I heard her pathetically limping up the stairs with her giant cast and I went into action." Alice smiled brightly at Burke. "I made you so hard that I was able to climb aboard and ride you. It felt so good to have you inside me. It was like old times. Annie walked in as we were going at it. You should have seen her face it was priceless. She looked shocked, stricken, and sick all at the same time. I relive that repeatedly and I have to admit it was one of my finest moments."

"And Cat?" he asked.

"Dead of course. I couldn't have cat hair on my clothes."

Burke groaned in disgust. Alice was sick in the head. It was going to take a lot of persuasion to get Annie back. No wonder she shot daggers at him. Placing his Stetson on his head, he went to the back door. He pulled open the screen door and turned around. "Be gone from here by the time I come home, or God help you," he warned letting the door slam louder than usual. He got on his horse. He needed to think this all through. He was in complete shock. If only he hadn't let Alice stay.

Annie would never forgive him. Why should she? From what Alice had said Annie went through hell. He didn't know how to begin apologizing to her. How could he possibly make things right between them? Maybe he should just wait until the baby was born. He had equal rights to the child—their child. Burke cursed as he looked to the heavens. He felt his face grow wet and realized that the wetness was from his own tears. He quickly wiped them away. A coward would wait and he wasn't a coward.

* * * *

The next day Annie received roses. She didn't want to open them; she already knew who sent them. Sitting there gazing at the box, curiosity finally got the better of her. She struggled to get out of her chair and she waddled her way to the kitchen table. She laid her hands on the box, feeling the silky smooth texture. There was a big red bow on it and it reminded Annie of better times. It reminded her of when Burke had proposed to her by flowers. A secret smile stole across her face as she remembered how happy and anxious she had been. The baby kicked and she laughed. Suddenly, she decided to open the box. As she lifted the top off, the scent of roses hit her. It was her favorite scent. The long stemmed red roses were perfect. She stroked the satiny petals as she admired their flawlessness.

There was a card, but she was reluctant to ruin the moment by reading it. Finally, she couldn't wait any more she had to know what it said. It simply read; *I was a fool, forgive me?* Annie smiled sadly. Tucking the card back into the box she walked away, needing some fresh air. Yes, he was a fool, she thought, but she felt as though she was the bigger fool.

Abruptly, she stopped herself from thinking negative thoughts. She just didn't have the energy to think about the past. It couldn't be changed, so she just wouldn't think about it. Annie laughed at herself. It was so much easier said than done, but she was determined to try.

She walked slowly and cautiously to her garden, feeling warmed and comforted by the Texas sun. It gave her pleasure to see that the acorn squash, the butternut squash, and her pumpkins finally taking shape. She wasn't able to do most of the gardening herself anymore. The last time she tried, she had the hardest time getting back up from the ground. Now she decided to forgo it for awhile. One of the men Clint had hired was blessed with a green thumb, so Annie knew that her garden was in capable hands.

She made her way to the corral to see the mares. They were beauties all right. Clint had a keen eye for horses and Jimmy McKeegan seemed a natural with them. Clint and Rheenie had finally moved into their new house. Annie had found a young girl to help him with Rheenie and to do some housekeeping. Noreen had mentioned to Annie that a girl in town needed her help. Apparently, her father had battered her and now he'd thrown her out into the street. The poor thing had nowhere to go, so naturally Noreen figured that Annie would take her in.

Her name was Ryelee and she was all of twenty years of age. She was all legs and limbs, a bit like a new filly. Her penny-bright hair was curly and it seemed unmanageable but it fit her, just as her freckles did. She was a bit awkward but she took to Rheenie right away and Rheenie was her constant shadow. Annie had a long talk with Clint about Ryelee and the living arrangements. He promised Annie that he wasn't in the market, wasn't even looking, and he would be the perfect gentleman. Annie knew all that before she approached him. It was good to know that her faith in him was well-placed though.

She laughed as one of the mares named Sybil came right to her nickering, nudging Annie hoping for a sugar cube. Clint didn't really approve, but Annie always brought her *girls* something. She looked as far as her eyes could see, loving her land and was surprised to see a lone cowboy silhouetted against the horizon watching her. He was far away, but Annie knew who it was. She would always be able to recognize her first love.

Annie greeted the other five mares, giving them each a sugar cube. Every time she looked up, Burke was still there, watching. Annie was trying to decide whether it gave her the creeps or made her feel good when Clint walked up to stand next to her.

He had been working desperately all week trying to negotiate a deal for a prize-winning stallion, to cover the mares. "Someone outbid us on King's Crown," he said disappointedly.

"You did your best. Clint. I don't doubt that. We'll just keep our eyes out for another stallion."

Clint gave her a weary smile. "I really wanted that horse. You're right though, we'll look for another."

"So who ended up with King's Crown?" Annie inquired.

Clint shook his head. "I don't know. I tried to find out, but I didn't have any luck."

She looked into his deep brown eyes and smiled. "How's Ryelee working out?"

Clint smiled as he watched one mare after another nudging Annie. "Giving them sugar again?"

Annie laughed there was no sense denying it. She just simply nodded her head. She enjoyed Clint's company.

"Ryelee and Rheenie are like two peas in a pod. She does a good job, but she won't even look at me. I think I make her nervous," he said

"Well, she's been through a lot," Annie answered, stroking Sybil's nose.

"I see you have a secret admirer," he stated nodding his head toward Burke.

Annie blushed. "Not so secret. He sent me roses this morning."

"And?" Clint prodded.

"And I don't know. I just finally made peace with myself. I'm sleeping better; I've stopped brooding over him. I just don't know if I can go there again. There was too much pain involved."

"I can identify with the pain part, but maybe you could give the guy a break. I've met him and he seems like a nice guy."

"Most guys are until they show their true colors," she commented bitterly.

"Looks to me that he's making an effort to win you back."

Annie looked at Clint. "I don't know if it's me or the baby he wants. Part of me cares and part of me doesn't." She looked away from Clint's penetrating eyes; she didn't want anyone to look into her heart. She didn't even know what was there. "I don't know how to deal with either choice."

Clint kissed her on the cheek. "One day at a time, Annie, one day at a time."

Annie watched him walk away. She could tell that he was speaking from experience. She looked back to see Burke, but he was gone. A feeling of loneliness filled her as she walked back to the house.

The next day yielded another delivery of flowers from Burke. The note was the same; *I was a fool, forgive me?* Annie smelled each rose as she arranged them in a vase. Burke was making it very hard to ignore him, but she was determined to stand firm. He had his life and she had hers.

It was important that she to talk to him. They needed to make decisions about the baby and visitation, but the whole thing depressed Annie. She never imagined that she'd be single mother, but here she was. Shaking her head, she tried to get rid of all of her negative thoughts, making a mental note to tell Mrs. Harvy to refuse any future deliveries of flowers from Burke. It made her feel things she didn't want to feel.

Grabbing a few apples, Annie walked outside to the mares. She loved to watch them frolic and play. Their antics always left her smiling. One by one, she feed them each an apple, admonishing a few of them for being greedy and trying to take more than their share. It amazed her how each had a distinctive personality. Some were more dominant than others. Annie always made sure that each horse got her share.

Looking out across her land she once again saw Burke on his horse, watching her. Part of her was annoyed and part of her was pleased. The pleased part scared her. She had promised herself that she wouldn't put herself in a position to get hurt again.

She had plenty of work to keep her busy. The busier, the better, as far as she was concerned. The nursery was her next project. Van had left paint chips and fabric swatches for her to look at. This was one time she wished that she knew the sex of the baby. She put aside the pinks and blues and tried to decide on the greens and yellows.

She had also sent for a catalog of baby furniture and absorbed herself in the many different styles and colors. Who knew that there was so many to choose from? Did she want a round crib or a regular one? Maybe she wanted the one that converted into a toddler's bed.

Annie smiled as she walked the room. Yellow, definitely yellow, she decided. It was a cheery color. She decided on green and yellow fabric with a butterfly and snapdragon pattern. Finally, she circled a maple crib in the catalog that converted into a toddler bed and the matching changing table and dresser.

Happily, she called Van and told him of her decisions. He promised to have the painters there the next day. For the rest of the day they looked at pictures of strollers, high chairs, and numerous other must-have baby items.

The next day Annie overheard Mrs. Harvy refusing the flower delivery. Once again, she felt torn. It was a feeling she would have to get used to she realized. She wanted Burke to have as much access to their child as he wanted. That meant that she would be seeing a lot of him. She needed to find a way to put the picture of Alice and Burke in bed out of her mind. There were many things that had hurt her, but seeing them together was the worst. The anger and betrayal ate at her.

The painters did a wonderful job. Their expert work pleased Annie. She had to sit outside most of the day, trying to avoid the paint fumes, which meant she saw Burke watching her again. This time he watched her for a very long time. Finally, he tipped his hat in her direction and rode away.

She wondered if he knew that she had his flowers sent back. Did it make him mad? She hoped that he got the message, and would stop.

Chapter Twelve

Annie felt that he must have gotten the message since she didn't receive a delivery the following day. A small feeling of disappointment managed to make its way into her consciousness. She'd gotten what she wanted, but it was cold comfort.

She was just finishing her lunch when she heard a truck drive up. Annie pushed herself out of the chair to find out who was on her property.

Mrs .Harvy came running in, smiling with excitement. "Your crib is here and it's already assembled. Oh, it's a beauty, Annie." She took Annie's hand and led her toward the nursery. "You need to tell them where you want it."

Annie was dumbfounded. She hadn't ordered the crib. She hadn't mentioned it to Van either. Walking into the yellow nursery, she was amazed. She couldn't take her eyes off the maple crib as she directed the movers. Finally she ran her hands over the smooth wood, smiling. It made the baby seem more reality and less abstract.

She wondered who sent it, but she had a feeling she knew. A surge of joy leapt into her heart. Burke cared about the baby. How he knew the exact crib she had wanted was no great mystery. She highly suspected that Mrs. Harvy has something to do with it. Mrs. Harvy was trying hard to look innocent and Annie didn't have the heart to take her to task.

This time Annie sat on the porch in anticipation of seeing her handsome cowboy ride up. She was not disappointed. She stared across the distance, this time with a warm feeling. It was silly really, to reconsider just because he bought a crib, but she couldn't help it. A lot of the bitterness slipped away. Her resolve to keep him at a distance was starting to wane. She tried to draw on her anger and her past suffering to fortify her, but it was useless. He tipped his hat to her and she hoped that he could see her smiling back.

The next day Annie was delighted with a delivery of a rocking chair. Surprisingly, it was the very one she wanted again. Annie laughed as she thought of Mrs. Harvy walking around with a secret smile on her face. But Annie played along, wondering aloud how Burke knew that she wanted that rocking chair.

The whole charade warmed her heart. She knew that the rocking chair was supposed to let her know that he cared about her too. She was melting toward him, but she still wasn't ready to let him back into her life. She had to protect her heart since she didn't think she could live through the pain again.

She did need to talk to him however. This baby was coming sooner rather than later and they had a lot to settle between them. She had heard that Alice left, but she wasn't going to believe it until she saw it. She deserved a faithful husband and she knew that sadly, Burke wasn't one.

Later would be a better time to think about the whole mess. She needed a nap. She had Lamaze class later in the afternoon and she wanted to be well rested. Sherry had agreed to be her labor coach. They had been to a few classes already and this class was the one everyone dreaded. It was the birthing film class. Annie wasn't looking forward to it, but ignorance would not be bliss in this case.

Annie was waiting for Sherry to pick her up for their class when the phone rang. It was Sherry. She was having car problems and asked if Annie could get her own ride, since she was just around the corner from the clinic. Annie agreed and asked Jimmy to take her into town. He dropped her off and told her to call when she needed to come home.

Annie walked into the class and was surprised when Sherry wasn't there already. Annie smiled at the other couples who were already present. She had been paranoid the first day since she was there with another woman instead of a husband, but upon seeing the group, she quickly felt at ease. There was every combination. There was a mother and daughter team, boyfriend and girlfriend teams, husband and wife teams and there was even a threesome of two men with their surrogate. She and Sherry had fit right in.

Annie looked at her watch, Sherry was really running late and the movie was about to begin. She was already on her mat with her pillow, having done her breathing exercises unaided. She didn't want to watch the miracle of birth alone.

"Miracle of pain, probably," she murmured to herself.

The lights soon dimmed and the movie started. It opened with a woman walking up and down the halls in a hospital waiting to dilate. Soon enough she was having contractions. Horribly painful ones as far as Annie could tell. She shuddered. Where was Sherry? She didn't want to watch any more of this movie. Frankly, it scared her.

So absorbed in the horror of pain she had hardly noticed when someone sat behind her, until she felt herself pulled back against a hard chest. Annie stiffened as she realized whose legs she sitting between. She didn't need to turn around. She knew Burke's scent. She had spent so much time making memories of him that she could never forget the scent of him, so masculine, all outdoors and sunshine. Her body began to tremble when he stroked up and down her arms. She wanted to pull away and run. She didn't want him here and she couldn't stop trembling. Finally, he put both hands on her belly.

Tears filled her eyes. Her emotions were all over the place. It felt good to have his hands on her especially since the baby was moving. There were times, so many times, she had wanted to experience this moment with him. She sighed and leaned back against him. When she looked back up to the screen, the woman was screaming in pain. Annie turned and pressed her face into Burke's arm, but she could feel him stroking her hair and she calmed.

Finally, it was over and the lights went on. She looked into Burke's sky blue eyes and saw tenderness, regret, and pain in them. She gave him a shy smile and put her hands over his. They were both holding the baby, together, she realized happily.

Class was over and Burke helped Annie get up.

"Did you get my presents?" he inquired.

"Y-yes I... uh. I did," she stammered.

"Did you like them?"

Annie nodded her head, still refusing to look at him. "Thank you."

"Annie, could we go somewhere and maybe have coffee and talk?" he asked softly.

Annie so wanted to say no, but deep down she knew that he deserved a chance. They needed to be civil to each other since they would be parents together. "Not the diner. I don't want anyone staring at me," she said.

"Not a problem, we could go to my place," he offered.

"W-w-w-what about Alice?" she sputtered.

"I kicked her out after that night at the movies. I don't tolerate liars."

"I just wish that I'd never met her."

Burke shifted on his feet. He wasn't sure what to say. "Me too."

She wished that she could be unaffected by his presence, but she wasn't. Her heart yearned to be one with him again. She didn't trust herself to look at him. She couldn't go through it all again, the broken heart, the betrayal, the humiliation. No, she had finally gotten back her self-esteem and she couldn't allow anyone to bring her down, ever again.

Annie finally looked at him. He looked so sincere and she felt like she was caving in. Her resolve to remain strictly co-parents was slowly trickling away. She remembered seeing him in bed with that slut of an ex-wife of his. It was a memory that she couldn't seem to shake. The look of pleading in his eyes was her undoing. She owed it to her baby to talk to its father.

"Okay, let's go to your place and talk," she said, a bit reluctantly. "You have to promise me that if I want to leave, that you take me home immediately, no questions asked."

"I can promise you that. I just want to talk, but if gets too much for you or the baby just say the word and I'll get you home as fast as I can," Burke replied seriously.

Annie didn't want to feel Burke's hands on her, but she needed help getting into his truck. The feel of his hands disturbed her almost beyond bearing. Her body automatically responded to him. Her larger breasts were actually aching for him.

The ride to Burke's ranch was silent. Annie kept thinking about how he'd have to help her out of the truck. She tried blaming it on hormones, but deep down she knew that she desired this man. That made him dangerous and she would have to be on guard. She needed to be able to think and speak clearly. They had a lot to work through especially for the sake of their baby.

The house was just the same. It was bittersweet to be here now. Some of its magic seemed to be gone. The building was the same, but Annie had changed. She wasn't the naive girl that she had been. She wasn't fanciful anymore. She had stopped thinking that a house could welcome her or that flowers could envelop her in joy. So much had happened in this house, and Annie wasn't crazy about spending time inside it.

She was so busy with her musings that she shrieked when Burke lifted her up into his arms and carried her to the front porch. She held on with her arms wrapped around his neck. His strength always amazed her. "Put me down!" she screeched, laughing. "I must weigh a ton."

Burke held her a bit tighter. "Really, Burke, put me down. I don't want to go into the house. Let's just sit here and talk."

Burke set her down gently onto the porch swing. "Sure if that's what you want," he agreed. "Let me get you a sweatshirt to put on it's getting a bit chilly."

Annie swung slowly back and forth on the swing. She didn't know why, but the stars seemed brighter here than at her place. There was a full moon dominating the night sky. It made Texas seem so big. There was a slight Texas breeze kicking up and Annie felt goose bumps on her arms. She was glad when Burke returned with his sweatshirt. Annie put it on, and felt instant comfort. It smelled like Burke.

* * * *

The swing jostled as Burke sat down beside her. He didn't know where to start. There was so much he wanted to say, so much he should say, but deep down he felt as though if he didn't get it right this time, he'd blow everything for good. If he had his way he'd sit right there on the porch swing with Annie on his lap, snuggling. He did find a bit of comfort that she hadn't refused to talk to him. He admired her. He sensed an inner strength that he hadn't noticed before.

He took a fortifying breath and dove right in. His head turned toward Annie, looking at her profile. He could see her stiffness and he understood. He wanted to take her hand, but somehow he knew that he shouldn't.

"I meant what I said in the card. I was a fool. I am a fool, and I'm sorry."

Annie still wouldn't look at him.

"The things I finally found out from Alice are diabolical. She planned on doing us both harm, and like a fool I never saw it coming. We'd still be together if I'd never let her into our lives. She manipulated me at every turn. She deceived me at every turn." Burke put his face in his hands. How was he going to explain everything and make it sound believable? Hell, he didn't even believe it and he lived through it. Burke sat up straight and looked at Annie. "Sonny and Alice were in cahoots to sabotage our marriage from the get go."

Annie gave him a quick look.

He told her about the deal Sonny and Alice had to steal her inheritance and how Alice double-crossed Sonny.

"They make me sick. Talk about being greedy! They tried to ruin my life for money?"

"There's more, much more and I should have believed you," Burke said, his heart in his throat. He explained about the trap and the kitten story. She was trembling so badly that Burke pulled her into his arms to offer comfort.

Rubbing her back, he went on to explain how the house and barn door ended up locked that night of the storm.

"I don't know if I want to hear anymore," Annie said with a sob. "Why didn't you ever believe me? I was your wife. I never did one thing to make you mistrust me!"

Burke looked at her. Her eyes were full of accusations and he knew he deserved it. He let her go and got up from the swing. Looking out at the dark Texas sky, he could see clouds rolling in. Turning around, he gazed at her. Even in grief, she was beautiful. It tore at his heart to know that he was as much to blame as Alice. He should have listened.

"I wish I knew the answer. Nothing made sense so I don't know. I just put it on the back burner and went back to what I do best, ranching."

Burke sat back down next to Annie, enjoying her nearness. "I'm a fool plain and simple. I let the past cloud the present and I just didn't give you the respect you deserved. You deserved my belief. You deserved my protection. I knew that you were no match for that bitch, but I only saw what I wanted."

Annie put her hand on his thigh. "I wish we could go back," she said wistfully. "I could never live here in this house again. The memories are sad and full of pain."

Burke sighed and went on.

Annie gasped when she heard that Alice had been responsible for her fall and she cried when she heard that Alice had drugged Burke in order to stage their sexual tryst.

Finally, Burke explained how he didn't know about the baby. He had never received any of her messages. He had yelled at her on the phone because Alice told him that Annie was harassing and threatening her. He told her how bitter and upset he was that she had left without saying goodbye and he apologized for all the harsh things he had said to her.

Tears ran down her face as she listened to Burke's bitter story. She knew that everything he had to say rang true. All the tears, the pain, the jealousy, and heartbreak were due to greed. It disgusted her. She was aghast that Alice and Sonny could be so devious, so callous. She felt Burke's arms going around her and she buried her face against his chest, trying to burrow closer longing to feel safe.

"I'm so sorry that I blew up at you for paying off my ranch. Noreen made me see the light on that one."

Annie was surprised. "Really, how did she do that?"

"She told me off, after I yelled at you. She told me just how generous you had been not only to her, but to the rest of the community." Burke sighed heavily.

"I always knew that Noreen was in my corner. I kept up with Weltworth gossip through her while I was in New York." Annie grew quiet as she listened to Burke's heartbeat.

Annie pulled away from him. "I saw you in bed with Alice. If you were drugged then how did you...well, you know?" She asked, and then held her breath, waiting for the answer. She closed her eyes, not wanting the answer. She knew what she had seen. It was something she had relived a million times.

"After she made you fall, she took full advantage of the fact that we couldn't sleep together," he explained. "She drugged me twice. She told me the first night she just sat in the room. She said that the second night she could hear you coming up the stairs." Burke turned red as he continued. "I guess she worked fast and hard to get me well, you know, able. I swear to you that I didn't even know she was in there. I was out like a light. If it's any consolation, she said that I deflated pretty fast."

Annie weighed everything he said. She could finally see that what he was saying was the truth. "I thought that you had broken my heart that night, but it was actually Alice's fault." She put her head on his wide shoulder. "She caused us so much pain, Burke. There were times that I'd thought I'd die from my broken heart."

"Me too, darlin', me too. It ripped my heart out when you left me. I didn't know why you left and it nearly killed me. It made me crazy, wondering what I had done to make you leave. It made me insane not knowing where you were. I missed you every second you were gone," he confessed.

Burke ran his hands up and down her back trying to comfort her. She began to wind down a bit when she felt the baby moving between them. It felt like the baby was doing some sort of acrobatics. Burke pulled away in awe and their eyes locked in a deep searching gaze. They mirrored each other's pain, regret, and love.

"I feel cheated out of being with you as our baby grew. I wanted to go through each step with you. I've missed so much because of my blindness to the truth."

"I've missed you every step of the way too, from the joyous first moment I realized I was pregnant. I cried for you during the morning sickness and I resented that you were never there during my doctor's appointments. The first sonogram nearly broke me. I was so alone."

"I know we have a lot to work on, but I don't want you to go one more step alone. I want to be there for both you and the baby. You are the only thing that brings me any type of pleasure. Hell, even the ranch didn't bring me peace after you left."

"I can't make any promises," she said sadly, shaking her head.

"I know, but I truly believe that in time we can make it right, make it work. I want to be a part of your life. I'm tired of looking at you from on top of my horse. I know I hurt you, but I want to be the one to put the smile back on your face."

Annie looked at him in wonder. His word spoke directly to her battered heart. His eyes seemed to be beseeching her to give him a chance. It was a chance that had been denied to both of them.

Her head felt as though it was spinning thinking of all the sleepless nights, all the days feeling devastated. So much wasted time. At least now, her anger was directed towards the right people, Alice and Sonny. Damn them both.

"What about my horse ranch? Are you okay with it? It used to be your land and I hope you'll like what I've done with it. I wanted to make it into something our child could inherit."

"Whatever makes you happy. It looks like a fine operation. You should be proud. I know that I am. It's a damn excellent legacy for our child."

His praise was a balm to her wounded soul. No one had ever been proud of her before and it touched her unlike anything else. It filled a void within her. It touched her heart and soul. It gave her bliss that was beyond any measure. What a rollercoaster of a day.

"Would you expect to run it?" she inquired. "I mean if we were to get back together?" Her face grew warm as she realized what she had just said. They hadn't talked about reconciling and here she was the first one to mention it. Maybe that wasn't in his plans. He said he wanted to be a part of her life, but he never mentioned what he meant by it. Maybe he wanted separate households. She hoped that he wanted her to marry him again. However, just talking like this and spending time together was going to have to be enough for now. She didn't need to borrow trouble.

Taking a deep breath, she decided to enjoy the moment and not worry about the future. "Well?"

Burke laughed. "No, darlin', those reins are all yours. I already have a cattle ranch to run. Besides I have it on good authority that you've surrounded yourself with some of the best in the business."

"Now would this same good authority have told you the exact crib I wanted?" she teased.

Burke smiled at her. "Mum's the word, but I do have to say her info is always correct. Her advice isn't half bad either."

"Well, God bless Mrs. Harvy. She's been like an angel on my shoulder. I don't know how I would have gotten through all this without her help."

"She's a fine woman all right." Burke agreed.

Burke got up from the swing and took Annie's hand. "There's something I want to show you." He helped her up.

Annie nodded. She wanted to see what he wanted to show her. She felt a bit shaky and unbalanced, more emotionally so. Still holding his hand, she followed as he led her down the porch steps. Now her curiosity was kicking in. She shot Burke a questioning look, but he only smiled at her mysteriously.

He led her to the paddock and told her to stay right there. She wasn't in the mood for games, but she did as he asked. Annie was amazed when Burke led out of the barn the most magnificent stallion she had ever seen. He was pure black and he was a beauty. Her eyes widened as she realized which horse this was.

"This isn't King's Crown is it?" she asked, her voice reflecting the excitement she felt.

Burke laughed. "The one and only."

"But how did you do it? I tried to buy him, but I wasn't fast enough with my offer," Annie asked, amazed that King's Crown was actually standing before her. She could hardly contain herself. She wanted to jump up and down, but she was afraid she'd fall.

"The owner and I go way back. I had to mortgage the ranch to buy him, but I figured that he was what I needed to help my wife fulfill her dreams, what I needed to be a part of her dream and a part of her future. You see, I love my wife to distraction and I want to give her happiness." Burke looked at Annie with his heart in his eyes. He waited for her reaction, barely breathing.

Annie stood there shocked. Joy filled her heart. He had mortgaged the thing that meant the most to him, his land. She looked into his blue eyes with adoration. She was falling in love with him all over again if that was possible. He was a man she could trust. He was a man that had integrity and lived by a code of honesty. She hadn't been wrong about him at all.

"Oh and one more thing, we're still married, Mrs. Dawson."

"Alice?" She asked.

"She made fake papers for me to see. I feel so brainless. I mean I knew her best. I knew just how cruel she could be. This whole fiasco is my fault," he admitted.

"She had me fooled too, Burke, but she didn't win. I love you, Burke. I have for so long."

Burke's grin was enormous as he opened his arms to Annie.

Annie gave a slight cry of happiness and threw herself into his powerful arms. She covered his face with kisses and the laid her head over his heart. It beat strong and fast, all for her. She had finally found a place where she belonged.

"Now what, Mr. Dawson? Do we still live in separate houses?"

"Well, Mrs. Dawson, my home is wherever you are."

Annie snuggled closer to him. "Right answer."

"Darlin', I want us to have the best ranch we can make for this little one here." He placed his large hand on her stomach.

Annie stepped back and looked at him. He looked so sincere. So much had happened this evening she felt emotionally drained. "Can we talk about this tomorrow?"

Burke frowned at her. "What's there to talk about?"

"I'm so tired, I can't even think right now. However, I do want to invite you to spend the night at my place. I'd like to have you hold me and the baby while we sleep and I want you there when we wake up," she explained smiling at him.

* * * *

Burke didn't even need to think it over. He immediately lifted Annie into his arms and headed for the truck. "I've been waiting for an invite to your place for a very long lonely time."

He gently put her in the passenger seat, reached over for the seat belt, secured her and kissed her cheek. "You do look weary," he observed, looking at the blue circles under her eyes. They hadn't been there earlier. The pregnancy must have tired her out. He'd have to talk to Mrs. Harvy about it. He wanted to make sure that Annie got all the rest and pampering she needed.

He felt buoyant driving to her house. He'd been waiting to get her into his arms for a long time. God knows he tried to resist her, he tried not to love her, but in the end, his heart won out. He was lucky to be getting a second chance.

Mrs. Harvy looked so pleased when Annie and Burke walked into the house. She didn't ask any questions she just made herself scarce.

Burke looked around and whistled. "Nice digs."

"Digs?"

"Yeah you know, nice place. They don't say digs in New York?"

"I've certainly never heard of it before, but thanks, I think," she said, taking his big work worn hand.

Annie led him into her bedroom. "I'm nervous, Burke."

Burke turned and tenderly framed her face with his hands. "My sweet, we are only going to sleep. I'm your husband you have no need to be nervous."

"I... I, well, I feel so fat!" she wailed.

Burke smiled into her eyes. "You are beyond beautiful. Don't forget that's my baby inside you, it's not fat."

"Okay, but I'm going to put on my night gown in the bathroom."

He smiled watching her grab a granny nightgown. He looked around the bedroom and noticed the rose décor. "A lot of flowers in this room," he said through the door.

"Is it too much?"

Hearing the pensiveness in her voice was endearing. "No, honey, you look great surrounded by roses."

The door jerked open. "You charmer."

"Get into bed, woman," he ordered.

"Gladly."

They got into bed and Burke drew her into the safety of his arms. She felt so good, so soft, so... so Annie, his Annie. She still smelled like the sweet smell of a rose. He kissed the top of her head as she snuggled against his shoulder. He could feel her tears fall on his skin. His heart twisted. "Please don't cry, Annie. I'm sorrier than you could ever know," he said softly.

"I'm just so happy that you are here. I've lain here night after night longing for you, missing you, being furious at you. I just can't believe we are in my bed together."

Burke felt his own eyes mist. "I'm glad to be here. I've had plenty of sleepless nights thinking about you too."

"Lay on your back," he said. "I want to feel the baby."

Annie turned onto her back, grabbed Burke's hand, and guided it to where the baby was kicking. "I think he'll be a soccer star with all the kicking," she said as she laughed.

"Or maybe she's a ballerina," Burke suggested.

"Does it matter to you whether it's a boy or girl?"

"Are you kidding? I'm just glad I get to be part of our child's life. Boy or girl it's a baby created from our love."

Tears rolled down her face again.

"You are the weepiest woman in all of Texas," he teased.

"I can't help it." She turned on her side to seek comfort in his brawny arms once again.

"It's okay, love, I don't mind." He stroked her back. Finally, he felt her relax and fall asleep. He knew that he was one lucky man to be here at all. He wanted to make plans for their future, but he knew that he still had some wooing to do. He didn't expect her to forget her hurt instantly.

* * * *

Annie woke to the bright sunshine a bit disappointed that Burke wasn't still with her, but she knew he'd probably been up for hours already, working the ranch. Being a ranch owner herself, she fully realized how much work was involved.

Smiling she caressed her stomach. "We're going to okay, little one. Your daddy is back."

"He sure is!"

"Burke what are you doing here? I thought you'd be off roping a cow or two."

Burke chuckled. "Actually I was, and then I had King's Crown brought over to your stables."

"Let me get dressed I want to see him." She eagerly got out of bed.

"Whoa there, little darlin'. Breakfast before horse."

Annie frowned at him, but she knew he was right. She needed to take care of herself for the baby's sake. "All right."

She wanted to laugh at the surprised look on Burke's face.

"I'll be right out."

It didn't surprise her that Burke was waiting in her room for her. "Okay let's go eat." She couldn't remember ever feeling so happy.

"Good morning," she said to Mrs. Harvy as she sat down at the kitchen table.

Mrs. Harvy looked from her to Burke with a secret smile. "Nice to see the two of you in the same room." She poured coffee for Burke and decaf tea for Annie. "Will we be having a permanent houseguest?"

Annie could feel Burke's sizzling gaze on her. She wanted to say yes. She wanted to have her dreams come true. It scared her to death that she might get hurt. She didn't think she'd survive a second time. In truth, it wasn't his fault. If Alice hadn't...

"We haven't talked about it yet," Burke replied.

"Oh, posh, what is there to talk about? Honestly, you two are as bad as two stallions in the same stall. The way I see it, you are partners in the ranch and partners as parents why not just hop into the hayloft and have at it."

Annie and Burke both burst out laughing at the same time. "Hop into the hayloft?" Annie choked out.

Mrs. Harvy looked flustered. "What's wrong with that? Might save your marriage. Lord knows you two don't know a thing about it. Now after you see that shiny new horse of yours, I'll have a picnic waiting for you to take."

"Yes, Ma'am," Burke replied as he took Annie by the hand and led her outside.

"Wait, you didn't eat! Here take these rolls." She handed them to Burke.

"Thanks."

Walking hand in hand felt so right to Annie. She felt as giddy as a child. "I can't wait to see him in the daylight."

"Wait don't walk so fast. I don't want you to fall," Burke admonished.

"Oh, pooh, let's just go."

"Did Annie Dawson, just say pooh?"

"Yes, I did, and I've learned more words if you'd like to hear them."

Burke threw his head back as the deep laughter rumbled out of him. "God, I love you!"

Annie gave him a sidelong glance and felt herself beaming. "Good—you'd better."

Annie was instantly distracted as she caught a glimpse of King's Crown. He was so beautiful. A beautiful black stallion, winner of many races, and he was hers. This was her hope for the future of her horse farm. He was going to produce outstanding foals. She was absolutely entranced by him.

She watched as Clint talked to him, getting him used to his new home. Clint smiled and waved. "I can't believe he's here."

Annie wished that she could climb up the rungs of the corral fence, but it was too cumbersome. "I'm going in."

Burke swept her off her feet before she could take another step. "Not with my child you are not!"

"You are not the boss of me!"

"Oh yeah?"

"Hell yeah!"

"Hey, hey let's keep it down, you're spooking King's Crown," Clint said in a soothing voice trying to calm the big stallion.

Annie turned her head so she was looking right into Burke's eyes and stuck her tongue out at him. She tried not to laugh as his eyes widened in surprise.

"Minx," he whispered.

"Bully," she whispered back.

"Wait until I hop in the hay with you," he said with a big grin on his face.

"It might have to wait until the baby is born, but cowboy, I can't wait to hop into the hay with you."

Burke kissed her holding her close.

"Mmmm. You can put me down now."

Burke put her down and they walked the rest of the way to the corral. Clint walked King's Crown over for Annie to pet. "I still can't believe that he's here. What do you think, Clint?"

"His offspring will be legendary, I can feel it."

"How goes it with Ryelee?" she asked. "I saw her on your roof the other day."

Clint shook his head. "I don't know what to do. She's so good with Rheenie, but I have to say she doesn't use the sense God gave her. She could have easily fallen off that roof and all for a Frisbee."

"Sounds like you have your hands full," Burke commented.

Clint smiled. "You're telling me? Half of me thinks she's a wonderful Nanny to Rheenie and she is a damn good cook too, but the other half has me praying hourly. I never know what she'd going to do next."

"Well, cowboy you'll get it all figured out. Rheenie seems happier than before."

"Yeah, that's the problem."

Annie and Burke laughed.

"Well, I'm going to put him out in the north pasture alone so he can mellow a bit. Have a good one."

"You too," Annie answered. She reached out and touched Burke's chest. "I can't believe you are here with me. It tore my heart to see you on your horse watching me. I felt so alone."

Burke put his hand over hers and moved them so that they were over his heart. "How should we do this? If I had my way I'd move in right away, but it's your call."

Annie looked into his blue eyes and saw all the love he had for her and it stunned her, it humbled her, and it delighted her to her very soul.

"I'm afraid, too," he whispered.

"Annie, please give me a chance, give us a chance. We have something good together."

Studying him, Annie couldn't think. Of course, she wanted to give him a chance, but what if it didn't work? What if? She couldn't live like this anymore. It was torture. "Hold me, Burke. I'm afraid."

Instantly cocooned in his embrace, she realized that with Burke she didn't need to be afraid. All she ever wanted was right here. "I love you."

"Your place or mine?" Burke asked in relief.

"I thought you liked my new digs," she teased.

"I do. I can run my side of the ranch from here. A few fences would have to come down and maybe a road built, but it's doable."

"Think so?" she asked eagerly.

"I know so. Now how about that picnic?" He took her hand and led her back to their house.

"I'll need a hat and probably a pillow because I don't think I'll be comfortable on the ground," Annie started to say.

The kitchen door opened and there stood Mrs. Harvy, her arms leaden with items. "And sunblock, and a blanket."

"What would we do without you?" Annie asked her dear friend.

"To tell you the truth I just don't know."

Burke laughed and took the items from Mrs. Harvy. "I'm moving in."

"'Bout time," she replied, with a twinkle in her eye.

"I think we should postpone the picnic." Annie felt her water break. "It's baby time."

She had to bite her lip when she saw the blood drain from Burke's face. Even Mrs. Harvy became flustered.

"Burke, I have a bag packed in my closet. Can you get it? Mrs. Harvy, call the doctor and let him know I'm on my way."

"People, am I the only calm one here? Get moving I have a feeling things are going to happen fast!"

Burke and Mrs. Harvy looked at each other and ran in two different directions. *Keystone cop time*, Annie thought as a sharp pain sliced through her. The baby wasn't due for another month, but she had a peaceful serene feeling. She wasn't sure, but it felt almost spiritual. Somehow, she knew that everything was going to be all right.

Burke came charging out of the house, scooped Annie up into his strong arms, and put her into the car. He looked shaken. She wished she could tell him it was going to be all right, but there was no way to know for sure.

"Hang in there babe, I'll get you there," he said trying to reassure her.

My hero, she thought. Another sharp pain sliced through her middle. "I don't want to worry you, but I need to get there now!" she cried out as yet another contraction happened.

By the time they arrived at the hospital, Annie was working on her breathing exercises— pant, pant, breathe. The Lamaze class mentioned thinking about a happy place. Right now, she wanted to grab her instructor around the neck and tell her that there was no such thing as a happy place! There were only places filled with labor pains.

She was wheeled to her room and immediately the nurse helped her change into a hospital gown. She was told that the doctor would be right in.

This time she screamed as another sharp pain rolled through her. "Burke! I need Burke!"

The on call doctor came in and told her that Burke was getting a gown on for the delivery room. "You're progressing rather quickly. I'm Doctor Potter. Don't you worry about a thing, were going to wheel you in now."

It was a whirlwind of activity. She pushed and pushed. Finally, when she thought she couldn't take it anymore the baby was born. Annie could see Burke looking worried. "Is something wrong with the baby?" she anxiously asked as she tried to sit up.

"We need to take care of you, lay back down," the doctor explained.

Tears were pouring out her eyes as she waited for an answer. She prayed and prayed. What if something was wrong? Was the baby all right? It seemed to take forever, but finally she heard the baby's cry. She cried out in relief. "Burke?"

He came to her side in his yellow hospital gown, reached over, and kissed her. "He's perfect, just perfect."

The nurse put the baby in her arms. Annie's heart expanded right then and there. He was beautiful with a touch of red hair on his head. The love, the instant bound took her by surprise. Smiling at Burke her eyes misted. "We are so blessed."

Burke put his finger in his son's hand and watched him grab hold of it. "We are. We really are."

Chapter Thirteen

Now Annie knew that the calm serene feeling she had right before her son's birth must have been some sort of sign from God. She'd never known such joy, such bliss. They had decided to name him Seth. It was an old Dawson name. They drove up to the house, which Burke had lovingly dubbed Dawson's Haven after he learned of all the strays that she had surrounded herself with.

The house welcomed her home. She could feel it. The roses swayed back and forth in the light Texas breeze. This was her home and she loved it. They would make wonderful memories here together. They would raise their family here and prosper.

Mrs. Harvey was standing on the porch, waiting, but she quickly ran toward the truck as it pulled up. Opening the passenger door, she gave Annie a quick going over and then laid her eyes on the baby. "Oh he's beautiful!" She took a tissue out of her apron pocket to dry her tears.

Annie smiled at her friend. "Yes he is. Let's get him into the house."

"Of course," Mrs. Harvy agreed as she stepped out of the way so that Burke could help both Annie and the baby out of the truck.

Annie had been worried that there would be many people at the house, but only Sherry and Ted were there. They immediately admired the baby.

Burke settled Annie on the couch and kissed her. He handed her the baby and stood back looking proud. He was going to be a great father. She just knew it.

"You just wait a few months and you'll have yours," Annie told Sherry. "I can't wait! Just imagine our children will play together and grow up together."

Sherry's hands immediately went to her blossoming middle. "I can't wait. Seth is such a doll! I'm so glad he's okay. When I heard that you went so early, well I'm just grateful."

"So are we," Burke said.

"I can see you're tired and this one needs to put her feet up. Congratulations to you both!" Ted said, pulling Sherry along.

"I'll be back soon so we can visit," Sherry said as she was led out the door.

"Mmmm, I have you two all to myself," Burke murmured. He sat on the edge of the couch. Annie could feel his intense perusal and it gave her a warm tingly feeling. She felt as though she was going to bust. She was so filled with joy.

"Okay! Now let's figure out the schedule and, well, there is a lot to talk about. So many things. For example, there is the bathing schedule, the feeding schedule, the stroller schedule. I know there must be more to plan," Mrs. Harvy said excitedly. "I also heard somewhere that you have to sign up for preschool as soon as the baby is born. The cleaning schedule will have to be changed. I can't vacuum while the baby is sleeping. Oh my, there is just so much!"

Annie laughed. "I think the way it works is that we plan around what Seth does. At least for the first month or so."

"The men will have to tread lightly. Maybe we should come up with some sort of signal to let them know to keep it down because the baby is sleeping. Hmmm, well, I'll think of something. Don't fret about it."

Seth began to cry and Annie felt the milk let down in her breasts. "Sounds like someone is hungry."

"I'll give you some privacy, then," Mrs. Harvy said a bit reluctantly. "So much to plan. Why didn't we think of these things before little Seth was born?"

Laughing as she opened her blouse, Annie looked at Burke. "I think that I'm going to have more help than I need."

"Perhaps," he said as he handed her their son. "I wonder how the men will feel about the quiet signal?"

"Don't worry, it'll be business as usual. They said at the classes I took that a little noise is good."

It embarrassed her at first to have Burke watch, but he seemed so amazed by the whole process that her embarrassment quickly waned.

"I've never seen anything so beautiful in my entire life," Burke told her in awe.

Annie smiled. "Well, be ready to be awed many times a day plus a few times at night," she teased.

"You give me so much joy. I love you, Annie, you are a strong courageous, smart, loving woman, and I'm so proud that you are my wife."

The look in his eyes almost made her cry. He was so sincere. He gave her what he promised—he gave her happiness. "Seth is going to be as handsome as you."

Burke smiled and watched as she finished feeding Seth. He even looked amazed when she changed his diaper. "I'm so thankful for what we have together. Look at this miracle of ours. He's a symbol of our love."

"Your sweet words are working wonders, Cowboy," she teased.

Annie had never felt so content, so happy, or so complete in her life. Later that night after they got Seth to sleep, she wanted to take a short walk to see the horses.

They walked together in the moonlight, holding hands. The sky was awash with sparkling stars and the breeze felt wonderful. It was hard to believe that she was a Texan now. Who would have believed it? It had been a wonderful day with Seth and Burke. Annie didn't remember ever smiling so much before.

Stopping at the corral, Burke turned her and cupped her face gently in his big hands. He looked into her eyes and then he gently kissed her. He took her into his strong, loving arms pulling her as close as she could get. Tears pricked the back of her eyes as she hugged him back.

She had done it. She had won this hardheaded cowboy's heart. He was her husband, her heart, and her haven.

THE END

About The Author

Kathleen Ball can easily read a book a day. She loves any type of Romance novel, especially Western Romances. Kathleen lives in Fort Worth, Texas with her wonderful husband. She has one son a Marine. Originally, from Rochester, New York, Kathleen finds Texas culture amazing. The more she immerses in it the more she likes it.

You can find updates on all of Kathleen's novels, releases and current works in progress at www.kathleenballromance.com

Secret Cravings Publishing
www.secretcravingspublishing.com

Made in the USA
Lexington, KY
02 March 2013